Smugglers' Reef

A Rick Brant Science Adventure Story

By John Blaine

Smugglers' Reef

Table of Contents

Chapter 1: Night Assignment

"Adventure," Rick Brant said, "is kind of hard to define, because what may be adventure to one person may be commonplace to another." He took a bite of cake and stretched his long legs comfortably. "Now, you take flying with Scotty. That's the most adventurous thing I do."

Mr. and Mrs. Brant and Jerry Webster looked at Don Scott, the object of Rick's jibe, and waited for his reply. Verbal warfare between the two boys was a usual feature of the evening discussions on the big front porch of the Brant home on Spindrift Island.

Scotty, a husky, dark-haired boy, grinned lazily. "You've proved your own point," he returned. "Flying with me is adventure to you but safe travel to anyone else. I'd say the most adventurous thing you do is drive a car."

Mrs. Brant, an attractive, motherly woman, poured another cup of coffee for Jerry Webster. The young reporter had started the discussion by stating wistfully that he wished he could share in some of the Brant adventures. "Why do you call Rick's driving adventurous?" she asked.

"The dictionary says so," Scotty replied. "One definition of adventure is 'a remarkable experience.'"

Hartson Brant, Rick's scientist father, grinned companionably at his son. "I agree with Scotty. Not only is Rick's driving a remarkable experience, but it fits the rest of the definition: 'The encountering of risks; hazardous enterprise.'"

Jerry Webster rose to Rick's defense. "Oh, I don't know. Rick always gets there."

"Sure he does," Scotty agreed. "Of course his passengers always have nervous breakdowns, but he gets there."

Rick just grinned. He felt wonderful tonight. When you came right down to it, there was nothing that matched being at home with the family in the big house on Spindrift Island. The famous island off the New Jersey coast was home for the scientific foundation that his father headed, and for the scientist members. It was home for Scotty, too, and had been since the day he had rescued Rick from danger, as told in The Rocket's Shadow . As junior members of the foundation, Rick and Scotty had been included in a number of experiments and expeditions. Rick wouldn't have missed a one of them, and if opportunity offered he would go

4

again with just as much eagerness. But it was nice to return to familiar surroundings between trips. More than once, during lonely nights in far places, his thoughts had turned to evenings just like this one with the family and perhaps a close friend like Jerry gathered on the porch after dinner.

Rick, Scotty, and Barbara Brant had only recently returned from the South Pacific where they had vacationed aboard the trawler Tarpon and had solved the mystery of The Phantom Shark. Barby had gone off to summer boarding school in Connecticut a few days later. Chahda, the Hindu boy who had been with the Brants since the Tibetan radar relay expedition described in The Lost City, had said good-bye to the group at New Caledonia and had returned to India. The scientists, Zircon, Weiss, and Gordon, were away doing research.

Suddenly Rick chuckled. "Speaking of adventure, I'll bet the biggest adventure Barby had on our whole trip to the Pacific was eating rosette saute at the governor's in Noumea."

"What's that?" Jerry asked.

"Bat," Scotty replied. "A very large kind of fruit bat. Barby thought it was wonderful until she found out what it was."

"I should think so!" Mrs. Brant exclaimed.

"It tasted good," Rick said. "Something like chicken livers." He grinned. "Anyway, I sympathized with Barby. I felt kind of funny myself when I found out what it was."

Hartson Brant, an older edition of his athletic son, looked at the boy reflectively. He knocked ashes from his pipe. "Seems to me you've been pretty quiet since you got back, Rick. Lost your taste for excitement? Or are you working on something?"

"Working," Rick said. "We scientists must never rest. We must labor always to push back the frontiers of ignorance." He put a hand on his heart and bowed with proper dramatic modesty. "I am working on an invention that will startle the civilized world."

"We will now bow our heads in reverent silence while the master tells all," Scotty intoned.

"I know," Jerry guessed. "You're working on a radar-controlled lawn mower so you can cut the grass while you sit on the porch."

"That's too trivial for a junior genius like Rick," Scotty objected. "He's probably working on a self-energizing hot dog that lathers itself with mustard, climbs into a bun, and then holds a napkin under your chin while you eat it."

5

"Not a bad idea," Rick said soberly. "But that isn't it."

"Of course not," Hartson Brant put in. "You see, I happen to know what it is, due to a little invention of my own--an electronic mind reader."

Scotty gulped. "You didn't tell Mom what happened to those two pieces of butterscotch pie, did you? I wanted her to blame it on Rick."

Rick asked unbelievingly, "An electronic mind reader? All right, Dad, what am I working on?"

"A device to penetrate the darkness."

Rick stared. His father had scored a hit. He demanded, "How did you know?"

"My new invention," Hartson Brant said seriously. "Oh, and one other clue. Yesterday morning the mail brought me a bill for a thousand feet of 16-millimeter infrared motion-picture film."

So that was it. Rick grinned. "I hope your new invention told you I asked the film company to send the bill to me and not to you."

"It did. The bill actually was addressed to the Spindrift Foundation, attention Mr. Brant. Since I didn't know which Mr. Brant was meant, I opened it. Don't worry, Rick. I'll let you pay it."

"Thanks, Dad," Rick said. "But don't make any sacrifices. You can pay it if you want to."

"Don't want to," Hartson Brant replied. "I haven't the slightest use for motion-picture film."

"Because Rick has the only motion-picture camera on the island," Scotty finished. He frowned at his friend. "Keeping secrets, huh?"

"I'm not sure it will work," Rick explained. He hated to brag about an idea and then have it turn out to be a dud. Consequently, he seldom mentioned that he was working on anything until he knew it would be successful.

"What does the film have to do with penetrating the darkness?" Jerry Webster inquired.

Rick caught the look of interest on his father's face. "Ask Dad," he said. "The electronic mind reader probably has told him all about it."

"Of course." The scientist chuckled. "Rick is planning to take movies at night without lights."

Jerry looked skeptical. "How?"

Rick stood up. "Long as we've started talking about it, I may as well show you."

The others rose too. As they did so, a shaggy little dog crawled from under

Rick's chair where he had been napping.

"Dismal and I will put the cake away," Mrs. Brant said.

At the sound of his name the pup rolled over on his back and played dead, his only trick. Rick bent and scratched his ribs in the way the pup liked best. "Go with Mom," he commanded. "Come on, the rest of you. Maybe I can get some free advice from the director of the Spindrift Foundation."

Hartson Brant smiled. "If you're looking for a technical consultant, Rick, my price is very reasonable."

"It would have to be," Rick admitted ruefully. "I've spent my entire fortune on this thing."

"The whole dollar," Scotty added.

The boys' rooms were on the second floor in the north wing of the big house. But where Scotty's was usually neat as a barracks squad room, the result of his service in the Marines, Rick's was usually a clutter of apparatus. Living on Spindrift Island with the example of his father and the other scientists to follow, it was natural that he should be interested in science. He was more fortunate than most boys with such an interest, because he was permitted to use the laboratory apparatus freely and his part-time work as a junior technician gave him spending money with which to buy equipment. Another source of revenue was his little two-seater plane. He was the island's fast ferry service to the mainland.

His room was neater than usual at the moment because he had not bothered to connect most of his apparatus after returning from the South Pacific. The induction heater that he used for midnight snacks was in a closet. His automatic window opener was not in use, nor was his amateur radio transmitter.

He opened a workbench built into one wall and brought out a motion-picture camera. It was a popular make with a type of lens mount that permitted fast switching of lenses. It used one-hundred-foot rolls of 16-millimeter film. He put the camera on the table, then from a cupboard he brought out what appeared to be a searchlight mounted on top of a small telescope.

"That's a sniper scope!" Scotty exclaimed.

Rick nodded.

"No reason why it shouldn't work very well, Rick," Hartson Brant said.

Jerry Webster sighed. "Excuse my ignorance. What's a sniper scope?"

"They were used during the last war," Scotty explained. He picked up the unit and pointed to the light, which was about the size and shape of a bicycle head lamp. "This searchlight throws a beam of black light. Rick would call it infrared.

Anyway, it's invisible. The telescope is actually a special telescopic rifle sight which will pick up infrared. You can use the thing in total darkness. Mount it on a rifle and then go looking for the enemy. Since he can't see the infrared, he thinks he's safe. But you can see him through the 'scope just as though he had a beam of white light on him."

"I see," Jerry said. "Where are the batteries?"

Rick brought out a canvas-covered case that looked like a knapsack. It had a crank on one side and a pair of electrical connections. "It's not a battery," he explained. "It's a small, spring-driven dynamo."

Jerry nodded. "I get it now. You rig this thing on the camera, which is loaded with infrared film. The film registers whatever the infrared searchlight illuminates. Right?"

"That's the idea," Hartson Brant agreed. "But it isn't as simple as that, is it, Rick?"

"Far from it. I have to determine the effective range, then I have to run a couple of tests to find out what exposure I have to use, and then I have to find the field of vision of the telescope as compared with the field of the lens. A lot depends on the speed of the film emulsion. That will limit the range. The searchlight is effective at eight hundred yards, but I'll be lucky if I can get a picture at a quarter of that."

"Where did you get the sniper scope?" Scotty wanted to know.

"By mail. I read an ad in a magazine that advertised a lot of surplus war equipment, including this."

"You might have said something about it," Scotty reproached.

Rick grinned. "You were too busy working on the motorboats. I knew you couldn't have two things on your mind at once."

Since the boys returned from vacation, Scotty had been overhauling the engines on the two motorboats which were used, along with Rick's plane, for communication with Whiteside, the nearest town on the mainland.

"I have a book downstairs that you'll find useful, Rick," Hartson Brant said. "It gives the comparative data on lenses. It may save you some figuring."

"Thanks, Dad," Rick replied. "I may have to ask your help in working out the mathematics, too. Anyway...." He stopped as the phone rang.

In a moment Mrs. Brant called. "Jerry, it's your paper."

"Something must have popped!" Jerry ran for the door.

Rick hurried after him, Scotty and the scientist following. The Whiteside

8

Morning Record , for which Jerry worked, must have had something important come up to phone Jerry on his night off.

In the library, Jerry picked up the phone. "Webster. Oh, hello, Duke. Where? Well, why can't one of the other guys cover it? Okay, I'll be on my way in a minute. How about a photographer? Hold the phone. I'll ask him." He turned to Rick. "Duke wants to know if you can take your camera and cover a story with me. A trawler went ashore down at Seaford."

Rick nodded quick assent. The little daily paper had only one photographer, who evidently wasn't available. It wouldn't be the first time he had taken pictures for Duke Barrows, the paper's editor.

"He'll do it. We're on our way." Jerry hung up. "Have to work fast," he said. "We start printing the paper at midnight."

"It's nine now," Scotty said.

Rick ran upstairs and opened the case containing his speed graphic, checking to be sure he had film packs and bulbs, then he snapped the case shut and hurried downstairs with it. Jerry and Scotty were waiting at the door.

"Don't stay out too late," Mrs. Brant admonished.

Dismal whined to be taken along.

"Sorry, boy." Rick patted the pup. "We'll be home early, Mom. Want to come along, Dad?"

"Not tonight, thanks," the scientist replied. "I'll take advantage of the quiet to catch up on my reading."

In a moment the three boys were hurrying toward the hook-shaped cove in which the motorboats were tied up. Although Spindrift Island was connected to the mainland at low tide by a rocky tidal flat, there was no way for a car to cross. The cove was reached by a flight of stairs leading down from the north side of the island. Elsewhere, the island dropped away in cliffs of varying heights and steepness to the Atlantic.

They ran down the stairs and got into the fastest of the two boats, a slim speedboat built for eight passengers. Rick handed Scotty his camera case and slid in behind the wheel. While Jerry cast off, he started the engine and warmed it for a moment. Then as Jerry pushed the craft away from the pier, he backed out expertly, spun the boat around, and roared off in the direction of the Whiteside landing.

"Let's have the story," Scotty shouted above the engine's roar.

"A fishing trawler from Seaford ran aground," Jerry shouted in reply. "Duke

9

figures it's an unusual story because those skippers have been going out of Seaford for a hundred years without an accident. There's no reason why one of them should run onto well-charted ground in clear weather."

Scotty squinted at the sky. "It's not exactly clear weather. There's a moon just coming up, but it's kind of hazy out."

"Yes, but you couldn't call it bad weather, either," Jerry pointed out. "Not from a seaman's viewpoint, anyway."

"Where did this trawler run aground?" Rick asked.

"Arm of land that extends out into the sea above Seaford," Jerry replied. "It's called Smugglers' Reef."

Chapter 2: Cap'n Mike

Jerry's car was an old sedan that had seen better days, but it could still cover ground at a good speed. The macadam highway unrolled before the bright head lamps at a steady rate while the beams illumined alternate patches of woods and small settlements.

There were no major towns between Whiteside and Seaford, but there were a number of summer beach colonies, most of them in an area about halfway between the two towns. The highway was little used. Most tourists and all through traffic preferred the main trunk highway leading southward from Newark. They saw only two other cars during the short drive.

Many months had passed since Rick's last visit to Seaford. He had gone there on a Sunday afternoon to try his hand at surf casting off Million Dollar Row, a stretch of beach noted for its huge, abandoned hotels. It was a good place to cast for striped bass during the right season.

"Smugglers' Reef," he said aloud. "Funny that a Seaford trawler should go ashore there. It's the best-known reef on the coast."

"Maybe the skipper was a greenhorn," Scotty remarked.

"Not likely," Jerry said. "In Seaford the custom is to pass fishing ships down from father to son. There hasn't been a new fishing family there for the past half century."

"You seem to know a lot about the place," Rick remarked.

"I go down pretty often. Fish makes news in this part of the country."

Scotty pointed to a sign as they sped over a wooden bridge. "Salt Creek."

Rick remembered. Salt Creek emptied into the sea on the north side of Smugglers' Reef. It was called Salt Creek because the tide backed up into it beyond the bridge they had just crossed. He had caught crabs just above the bridge. But between the road and the sea there was over a quarter mile of tidal swamp, filled with rushes and salt-marsh grasses through which the creek ran. At the edge of the swamp where Salt Creek met Smugglers' Reef stood the old Creek House, once a leading hotel, now an abandoned relic.

A short distance farther on, a road turned off to the left. A weathered sign pointed toward Seaford. In a few moments the first houses came into view. They

11

were small, and well kept for the most part. Then the sedan rolled into the town itself, down the single business street which led to the fish piers.

A crowd waited in front of the red-brick town hall. Jerry swung into the curb. "Let's see what's going on."

Rick got his camera from the case, inserted a film pack, and stuffed a few flash bulbs into his pocket. Then he hurried up the steps of City Hall after Jerry and Scotty. Men, a number of them with the weathered faces of professional fishermen, were talking in low tones. A few looked at the boys with curiosity.

An old man with white hair and a strong, lined face was seated by the door, whittling on an elm twig. Jerry spoke to him.

"Excuse me, sir. Can you tell me what's going on?"

Keen eyes took in the three boys. "I can. Any reason why I should?" The old man's voice held the twang peculiar to that part of the New Jersey coast.

"I'm a reporter," Jerry said. "Whiteside Morning Record ."

The old man spat into the shrubbery. "Going to put in your paper that Tom Tyler ran aground on Smugglers' Reef, hey? Well, you can put it in, boy, because it's true. But don't make the mistake of calling Tom Tyler a fool, a drunkard, or a poor seaman, because he ain't any of those things."

"How did it happen?" Jerry asked.

"Reckon you better ask Tom Tyler."

"I will," Jerry said. "Where will I find him?"

"Inside. Surrounded by fools."

Jerry pushed through the door, Rick and Scotty following. Rick's quick glance took in the people waiting in the corridor, then shifted to a young woman and a little girl. The woman's face was strained and white, and she stared straight ahead with unseeing eyes. The little girl, a tiny blonde perhaps four years old, held tightly to her mother's hand.

Rick had a hunch. He stopped as Jerry and Scotty hurried down the corridor to where voices were loud through an open door. "Mrs. Tyler?" he asked.

The woman's head lifted sharply. Her eyes went dark with fear. "I can't tell you anything," she said in a rush. "I don't know anything." She dropped her head again and her hand tightened convulsively on the little girl's.

"Sorry," Rick said gently. He moved along the corridor, very thoughtful, and saw that Jerry and Scotty were turning into the room from which voices came. Mrs. Tyler might have been angry, upset, tearful, despondent, or defiant over the loss of her husband's trawler. Instead, she had been afraid in a situation that did

12

not appear to call for fear.

He turned into the room. There were about a dozen men in it. Two were Coast Guardsmen, one a lieutenant and the other a chief petty officer. Two others were state highway patrolmen. Another, in a blue uniform, was evidently the local policeman. The rest were in civilian clothes. All of them were watching a lean, youthful man who sat ramrod straight in a chair.

A stocky man in a brown suit said impatiently, "There's more to it than that, Tom. Man, you've spent thirty years off Smugglers'. You'd no more crack up on it than I'd fall over my own front porch."

"I told you how it was," the fisherman said tonelessly.

Rick searched his face and liked it. Tom Tyler was perhaps forty, but he looked ten years younger. His face was burned from wind and sun, but it was not yet heavily lined. His eyes, gray in color, were clear and direct as he faced his questioners. He was a tall man; that was apparent even when he was seated. He had a lean, trim look that reminded Rick of a clean, seaworthy schooner.

The boy lifted his camera and took a picture. The group turned briefly as the flash bulb went off. They glared, then turned back to the fisherman again.

The town policeman spoke. "You know what this means, Tom? You not only lost your ship, but you're apt to lose your license, too. And you'll be lucky if the insurance company doesn't charge you with barratry."

"I've told you how it was," Captain Tyler repeated.

The man in the brown suit exploded. "Stop being a dadblasted fool, Tom! You expect us to swallow a yarn like that? We know you don't drink. How can you expect us to believe you ran the Sea Belle ashore while drunk?"

"I got no more to say," Tyler replied woodenly.

Jerry turned to Rick and Scotty and motioned toward the door. Rick led the way back into the corridor. "Getting anything out of this?" he asked.

"A little," Jerry said. "Let's go out and talk to that old man."

"Lead on," Scotty said. "I've always wanted to see a real news hound in action."

Rick dropped the used flash bulb into a convenient ash tray, replaced it with a new one, and reset the camera. At least he had one good picture. Tom Tyler, framed by his questioners, had looked somehow like a thoroughbred animal at bay.

Outside the door, the old man was still whittling. "Get a real scoop, sonny?" he asked Jerry.

"Sure did," Jerry returned. He leaned against the doorjamb. "I didn't get your name."

"Didn't give it."

"Will you?"

"Sure. I ain't ashamed. I'm Captain Michael Aloysius Kevin O'Shannon. Call me Cap'n Mike."

"All right, Cap'n Mike. Is it true Captain Tyler stands to lose his master's license and may be even charged with deliberately wrecking the ship?"

"It's true.

"He says he was drunk."

"He wasn't."

"How do you know?"

"I know Tom Tyler."

"Then how did it happen?"

Cap'n Mike rose and clicked his jackknife shut. He tossed away the elm twig. "You got a car?"

"Yes."

"Let's take a ride. You'll want to see the wreck, and I do, too. We can talk on the way."

The boys accepted with alacrity. Rick and Scotty sat in the back seat; the captain rode up front with Jerry. At the old man's direction, Jerry drove to the water front and then turned left.

"I'll start at the beginning," Cap'n Mike said. "I've had experience with reporters in my day. Best to tell 'em everything, otherwise they start leaping at conclusions and get everything backwards. Can't credit a reporter with too many brains."

"You're right there," Jerry said amiably.

Rick grinned. He had seen Jerry in operation before. The young reporter didn't mind any kind of insult if there were a story in the offing. Rick guessed the newspaper trade wasn't a place for thin skins.

"Well, here're the facts," the captain continued. "Tom Tyler, master and owner of the Sea Belle, was coming back from a day's run. He'd had a good day. The trawler was practically awash with a load of menhaden. In case you don't know, menhaden are fish. Not eating fish, but commercial. They get oil and chicken and cattle feed from 'em, and the trawlers out of this port collect 'em by the millions of tons every year."

14

"We know," Jerry said.

"Uhuh. As I said, the trawler was full up with menhaden. Tom was at the wheel himself. The rest of the crew, five of them, was making snug. There was a little weather making up, but not much, and not enough to interfere with Tom seeing the light at the tip of Smugglers' Reef. He saw it clear. Admits it. Now! All you need do is give the light a few fathoms clearance to starboard. But Tom Tyler didn't. And what happened?"

"He ran smack onto the reef," Scotty put in.

"He surely did. The crew, all of 'em being aft, didn't see a thing. First they knew they were flying through the air like a bunch of hooked mackerel and banging into the net gear. One broken arm and a lot of cuts and bruises among 'em. The trawler tore her bottom out and rested high and dry, scattering fish like a fertilizer spreader. Tom Tyler said he took one drink and it went to his head."

The old man snorted. "Bilge! Sheer bilge! He said hitting the reef sobered him up."

"Maybe it did," Jerry ventured.

"Hogwash. There wasn't a mite of drink on his breath. And what did he drink? There ain't nothing could make an old hand like Tom forget where a light was supposed to be. No, the whole thing is fishy as a bin of herring."

The boys were silent for a moment after the recital, then Rick blurted out the question in his mind. "What's his wife afraid of?"

The captain stiffened. "Who says she's afraid?"

"I do," Rick returned positively. "I saw her."

"You did? Well, I reckon you saw right."

"Maybe she's afraid of Tyler's losing his way of making a living," Scotty guessed.

Rick shook his head. "It wasn't that kind of fear."

The sedan had left the town proper and was rolling along the sea front on a wide highway. This was Million Dollar Row. In a moment Rick saw the first of the huge hotels that had given the road its name. It was called Sandy Shores. Once it had been landscaped, and probably beautiful. Now, he saw in the dim moonlight, the windows were shuttered and the grounds had gone back to bunch grass. The paint had peeled in the salt air and there was an air of decay and loneliness around the dark old place.

Extending up the drive were the Sea Girt, the Atlantic View, Shore Mansions, and finally, the Creek House. All were in similar condition. These hotels had been built in the booming twenties when the traditional sleepiness of Seaford had been disturbed by a rush of tourists. Then had come the business depression of the thirties and the tourists had stopped coming. They had never started again. The hotels, too expensive to operate and useless as anything but hotels, had been left to rot. Briefly, during World War II, they had served as barracks for a Coast Guard shore patrol base, but that activity was long past now, and they had been left to decay once more.

There were a number of cars on the road, going both ways. Captain Mike remarked on the fact. "They're curious about the wreck. Usually not a car moves on this road."

As they approached Smugglers' Reef, the cars got thicker. Then Rick saw lights in the massive Creek House. It was one of the biggest of the hotels, and it had been the most exclusive. It had its own dock on Salt Creek, and it was protected from prying eyes by a high board fence. Two rooms on the second floor were lit up.

"It's occupied," Cap'n Mike affirmed. "Family name of Kelso is renting it. Claim they need the salt air and water for their boy. He's ailing."

"Must be a big family," Scotty said.

"Oh, they don't use all of it. Just a couple of bedrooms and the kitchen. No one knows much about 'em and they don't seem to work at anything. City folks. Keep to themselves."

Rick guessed from the note of irritation in Cap'n Mike's voice that he resented the Kelsos' evident desire for privacy. Probably he had tried to satisfy his curiosity about them and had been rebuffed.

Jerry pulled up in front of the hotel and stopped the car. The boys piled out, anxious for a glimpse of the trawler. Rick crossed the road and looked out to sea.

Smugglers' Reef was a gradually narrowing arm of land that extended over a quarter mile out into the sea. In front of the hotel it was perhaps two hundred yards wide. Then it narrowed gradually until it was little more than a wall of piled boulders. On its north side, Salt Creek emptied into the sea. Beyond the creek was the marsh with its high grasses.

At the far tip of the reef, a light blinked intermittently. That was the light Tyler had failed to keep on his starboard beam. A few hundred feet this side of it was a moving cluster of flashlights. It was too dark to make out details, but Rick guessed the lights were at the wrecked trawler.

"Got your camera?" Jerry asked.

16

Rick held it up.

"Then let's go. Time is getting short and I have to get the story back."

With Cap'n Mike leading the way, surprisingly light on his feet for his age, the boys made their way out along the reef. A short distance before they reached the wreck they passed a rusted steel framework.

"Used to be a light tower," Cap'n Mike explained briefly. "They put up the new light on the point a few years back and put in an automatic system. This light had to be tended."

At the wreck they found almost two dozen people. Flashlights picked out the trawler. It had driven with force right up on the reef, ripping out the bottom and dumping thousands of dead menhaden into the water. They lay in clusters around the wreck, floating on the water in silvery shoals. The air was heavy with the reek of fish and spilled Diesel fuel.

There was little conversation among those who had come to visit the wreck. When they did talk, it was in low tones. Rick thought that was strange, because anything like this was usually a field day for self-appointed experts who discussed it in loud tones and offered opinions to all who would listen. Then, as he lifted his camera for a picture, he saw the men look up, startled at the flash. He saw them turn their backs quickly so their faces would not be seen if he were to take another picture.

He sensed tension in the air, and his lively curiosity quickened. This was no ordinary wreck. Something about it had brought fear. Or was it that the fear had brought the wreck?

"Let's go," Jerry said. "Got a deadline to make."

*   *   *   *   *

Rick lay awake and stared through the window at the darkness. Jerry had the pictures and story and there seemed to be nothing else to do except to cover the hearing that would follow. The results were a foregone conclusion. Trawler skipper admits he ran ship aground while drunk. Case closed.

Again Rick saw the fear written on Mrs. Tyler's face. Again he sensed the tension among the men who gathered at the wreck. And he believed Cap'n Mike had left some things unsaid in spite of his apparent frankness.

"Scotty?" he whispered.

Scotty's voice came low through the connecting door. "I'm asleep."

"Same here. Let's go fishing tomorrow."

"Okay. I know where the blackfish will be running."

17

"Do you? Where?"

Rick grinned sleepily as Scotty's whisper came back.

"Off Smugglers' Reef."

Chapter 3: The Redheaded Kelsos

The Spindrift motor launch rolled gently in the offshore swell as the New Jersey coast slid by off the starboard beam. Behind the wheel, Rick steered easily, following the shore line. In the aft cockpit, Scotty prepared hand lines for the fishing they planned to do to keep up appearances.

Their decision to revisit Smugglers' Reef had been made on the spur of the moment. The case of the wrecked trawler was none of their business, and Rick had learned in the past that it was a good idea to keep his nose out of things that didn't concern him. But he could no more resist a mystery than he could resist a piece of Mrs. Brant's best chocolate cake. He watched the shore line as the launch sped along and tried to assure himself that a little look around wasn't really sticking his nose into the case. After all, it wouldn't hurt to satisfy his curiosity, would it?

Scotty came forward and joined him. "All set. We ought to find some fish right off the tip of the reef. If you intend to do any fishing, that is."

"Of course we'll fish," Rick said. "What else did we come here for?"

"Nothing," Scotty agreed. "This is a fishing expedition in the truest sense of the word."

Rick looked at his pal suspiciously. "What was behind that remark?"

Scotty chuckled. "Are you fooling yourself? Or are you trying to fool me?"

Rick had to laugh, too. "Okay. Let's admit it. We're so used to excitement that we have to go fishing for it if none comes our way. But seriously, Scotty, this is none of our business. The local officials can handle it without any help from us. So let's not get too involved."

Scotty leaned back against the seat and grinned lazily. "Think you can take your own advice?"

"I think so," Rick said, with his fingers crossed.

Scotty pointed to a low line ahead. "There's the reef. See the light on the tip?"

"Couldn't very well miss it," Rick said. The light was painted with red and white stripes and it stood out sharply against the sky. He gave Scotty a side glance. "What did you make out of all that talk last night? Think Captain Tyler ran on the reef purposely?"

Scotty shook his head. "He didn't strike me as a thief, and that's what he'd have to be to wreck his trawler on purpose."

"I liked his looks, too. Then Cap'n Mike said he didn't drink, so his statement that he was under the influence of liquor wouldn't hold water, either. What's the answer?"

"If we knew, would we be here?" Scotty waved at the shore. "How far does this stuff extend?"

The water ended in an almost solid wall of rushes and salt-marsh growth that would be far above even a tall man's head if he stood at sea level. Now and then a small inlet appeared where the water flowed too rapidly for plant life to grow.

"There's about a mile of the stuff," Rick said. "It stops at the reef. I'm not sure how wide it is, but I'd guess it averages a quarter of a mile. It's called Brendan's Marsh, after an old man who got lost in it once. It was over a week before he was found."

They were approaching the reef at a good clip.

"What do we do first?" Scotty asked.

Rick shrugged. He had no plan of action. "Guess we just sort of wander around and wait for a bright idea to hit us."

"Lot of other people with the same idea, I guess." Scotty nodded toward the reef.

Rick saw a number of figures moving around the wreck of the trawler. "Wonder who they are?"

"Probably a lot of folks who are just curious--like two in this boat. And I wouldn't be surprised if the law was doing a little looking around by daylight, too."

"We'll soon see." Rick turned the launch inshore as they approached the reef. "Let's tie up at the Creek House dock. Then we can walk down the reef and join the rest."

"Suits me."

Rick rounded the corner of the salt marsh and steered the launch into the creek, reducing speed as he did so. On their right, the marsh stretched inland along the sluggish creek bank. On their left, the high old bulk of the Creek House rose from a yard that was strewn with rubble and years' accumulation of weeds and litter. A hundred yards up the creek was the gray, rickety piling of the hotel dock.

"That's it," Rick said.

Scotty went up to the bow and took the bow line, ready to drop it over a piling.

Rick started a wide turn that would bring him into the dock, then cut the engine. The launch slowed as it lost momentum and drifted into place perfectly.

"Hey! Get out of there!"

Both boys looked up.

Coming from the hotel's side door on a dead run was a stocky youth of about their own age. He was between Rick and Scotty in height, and he had hair the color of a ripe carrot. Swinging from one hand was a rifle.

"Is that hair real or has he got a wig on?" Scotty asked.

"It's real," Rick returned. His forehead creased. The dock had never been considered private property--at least not since the hotel was abandoned. He waited to see what the redhead wanted.

The boy ran down the loose wooden surface toward them, his face red and angry. "Get that boat out of here!"

Rick looked into a pair of furious eyes the color of seaweed, set above a wide nose and thin mouth.

"Why?" he asked.

"This is private property. Cast off."

"Where's your sign?" Scotty asked.

The boy grinned unpleasantly. "Don't need a sign." He patted the stock of his rifle. "Got this."

"Plan to use it?" Scotty asked calmly.

"If I have to. Now cast off those lines and get out."

Rick's temper began to fray a little. "You're using the wrong tone of voice," he said gently. "You should say 'I'm terribly sorry, fellows, but this is private property. Do you mind tying up somewhere else?' Ask us nicely like that and we'll do it."

The redhead half lifted the rifle. "Wise guy, huh? I warned you. Now cast off those lines and get out." He dropped his hand to the lever of the rifle as though to pump a cartridge into place.

Scotty tensed. He said softly, "Get gay with that rifle and I'll climb up there and feed it to you breech first."

Rick saw the color rise to the boy's face and the muscles in his throat tighten. "Easy, Scotty," he said warningly. He knew, as Scotty did, that no normal person would wave a rifle at anyone for mere daytime accidental trespassing, but he had

21

a hunch the young carrot-top would not react normally.

"Jimmy!"

The three of them looked to the hotel as the hail came. A big man with red hair several shades darker than the boy's was waving from the side door of the Creek House. He walked toward them rapidly.

"Okay, Pop," Carrottop called. "I told 'em to get out."

As the man approached, Rick saw that there was a strong resemblance between the man and the boy. Evidently they were father and son. The man had the same thin lips, the same seaweed-green eyes. His face was almost square. It was a tough face, Rick thought.

The newcomer looked at his son and jerked his thumb toward the hotel. "Okay, Jimmy, get into the house."

The boy turned and walked off without a word.

The man surveyed Rick and Scotty briefly. "Don't mind Jimmy. He was probably rude, and I'm sorry for it. But this is private property and I can't allow you to tie up here." He motioned to the high board fence along the front of the hotel. The fence ran down to the edge of the creek. "Anywhere this side of the fence is private."

Rick nodded. "It didn't use to be. That's why we tied up here. I'm sorry, Mr...."

"Kelso. I rented the place a few weeks ago. Haven't had time to get signs up yet."

"We'll shove off right away, Mr. Kelso. Sorry we intruded."

"Okay."

Rick started the engine, threw the launch into reverse, and backed out.

Scotty sat down beside him. "How about that?"

"Funny," Rick said. "Didn't Cap'n Mike say a family named Kelso had taken the hotel because their little boy was sick and needed fresh air?"

"That's what he said," Scotty affirmed. "Do you suppose that was the sick little boy?"

"If he's sick," Rick said grimly, "it's trigger fever. I think he'd like to take a shot at someone."

"It would sure be an effective way of discouraging trespassers. Why do you suppose they crave privacy so much?"

"Beats me," Rick said. "We'll have to ask Cap'n Mike."

The launch passed the edge of the Creek House fence and came to a strip of sandy beach. The road ended a few feet from the beach. A number of cars were parked in the area, and along Smugglers' Reef were the occupants, most of them standing around the wreck.

"I'll run the launch in as far as I can," Risk directed, "then you jump ashore with the anchor."

"Okay." Scotty went forward and took the small anchor from its lashings, making sure he had plenty of line. As Rick pushed the bow of the launch into shallow water until it grated on the sand, Scotty jumped across the six feet of open water to the beach.

Rick took the keys from the ignition and joined him. Together they pulled the launch in a foot or two more, then dug the anchor into the sand. It would hold until the tide changed.

"Let's go look at the wreck," Scotty said.

Rick nodded. "Afterward, I think we'd better go look up Cap'n Mike. I have some questions I want to ask him."

"About what?"

"Something he said last night. And about the Kelsos."

They reached the old light tower and paused to examine it. Salt air had etched the steel of the frame badly. The tower was almost forty feet high, about twice as tall as the present light. At its top had been a wooden platform where the lightkeeper had once stood to care for the light. A rusty metal ladder led up one side of the tower to where the platform had been.

Rick wondered why the authorities had abandoned the tower in favor of the smaller light at the very tip of the reef and decided it probably was because having the warning signal at the very point was more practical. That way, a ship needed only to clear the light without worrying about how far away from the light it had to pass.

"Let's go," Scotty said. "Nothing interesting about this relic."

They joined the group of men at the wreck of the Sea Belle and saw that the wreck was being inspected, probably by the insurance people. A question to one of the watchers affirmed the guess. Rick asked, "What do they expect to find?"

"Search me."

Scotty nudged Rick. "We won't have to look far for Cap'n Mike. There he is."

The old man was seated on a rock, whittling at a twig. Seemingly, he paid no attention to anything going on. Now and then he looked out to sea, but mostly he paid attention to his whittling.

Rick walked over, Scotty behind him. "Good morning, Cap'n Mike."

"'Morning, boys."

"Remember us?"

"Sure do. Where's the reporter?"

"He's not with us. We came down to do a little fishing."

Bright eyes twinkled at them. "Fishing, eh? What kind?"

"We thought we might get some blackfish at the end of the reef," Scotty replied.

"You might at that," Cap'n Mike said. "You might gets crabs off the end of the Creek House pier, too, if Red Kelso would let you try. Did you ask him?"

Rick grinned. Cap'n Mike might not seem to be paying attention, but evidently he didn't miss much.

"We didn't ask him," he said. "Maybe we didn't even see him." He knew Cap'n Mike could have seen the boat vanish upcreek and return, but he wouldn't have been able to see past the fence.

"Maybe you didn't," the old captain conceded. "But you sure saw somebody, and it had to be Kelso or that boy of his."

"Why do they want so much privacy?" Scotty demanded.

Cap'n Mike ignored the question. "You really got any fishing gear in that launch?"

"Hand lines," Rick said.

"That's good as anything. Now, I always say a man can't think proper in a mob like this. Too distracting. So let's go fishing and do some thinking. What say?"

Rick's glance met Scotty's. Cap'n Mike had his own way of doing things. They had nothing to lose by humoring him.

"Let's go," Scotty said.

As they passed the wreck, Rick stopped for a moment to look at it again. The air was even heavier than the night before with the reek of dead fish. They were scattered along the reef in shoals ten feet wide. By daylight he could see that the trawler was finished. She had broken her back and torn out a good part of her bottom. She must have been really making knots to hit like that.

"Cap'n, exactly what was the weather like when Tom Tyler hit?" Rick asked.

"Not bad. Visibility might have been less than real perfect, but it wouldn't have interfered with him seeing the light."

"Would it have interfered with him seeing the reef if the light had been out?"

"I reckon it would. Until he was right on it, anyway."

Rick turned the information over in his mind. "Were any other trawlers out last night?"

"Plenty. The Sea Belle was first in, but the rest were right behind. The light was burning, all right. I thought of that, too, son."

"My name is Rick Brant. This is Don Scott. We call him Scotty."

"Knew you both," Cap'n Mike said. "I subscribe to the paper your friend writes for. Seen your pictures couple of times. Didn't you just get back from somewhere?"

"The South Pacific," Scotty said.

"Used to sail those waters. Reckon things have changed some."

"The war changed the islands," Scotty told him. "Especially...." he stopped suddenly and took Rick's arm. "Look."

The elder Kelso was standing in front of the launch.

"What do you suppose he's after?" Rick asked.

Before Scotty or Cap'n Mike could think up an answer, Kelso turned and walked back along the beach. There was a foot or two of space between the water of the creek and the hotel fence. The redheaded man slipped through it and vanished from sight.

"I'll bet he came out just to look the boat over," Scotty guessed, "and there's only one reason I can think of why he'd do that. He wanted to see if he could find out more about us."

"Unless he admired the launch and wanted a closer look at it," Rick added.

Cap'n Mike snorted. "Red Kelso's got no eye for beauty, in boats, anyway."

"Then my guess must have been right," Scotty said.

"Right or wrong," Cap'n Mike retorted, "I can't say's I like it. I wish you boys had talked to me before you decided to invade Salt Creek!"

Chapter 4: A Warning

Cap'n Mike tested his line, then gave a sharp tug. He hauled rapidly and lifted a three-pound blackfish into the boat.

"Practically a minnow," he said.

"Did we come out here to fish or to talk?" Rick asked. They were anchored a few hundred yards off the reef tip and had been for almost an hour. In that time Cap'n Mike had made a good haul of four blacks, one flounder and a porgy. Rick and Scotty had caught two blacks apiece.

There was a definite twinkle in Cap'n Mike's eyes. "Came to talk," he said. "But the fish are biting too good. Better fish while the fishing's good. Time enough to talk later."

"Time enough for fishing later, you mean," Rick retorted. "Hauling in blackfish isn't going to find out why the Sea Belle was wrecked."

"Got the answer to that already," Cap'n Mike said.

Rick and Scotty stared. "You have?" Rick asked incredulously.

"Stands to reason. Didn't you tell me you knew Mrs. Tyler was scared?"

"Yes, but what...."

"Well, Tom is scared, too. He wasn't, until the Sea Belle was wrecked, but he sure is now. That's why he's sticking to that story of his instead of telling the truth."

"What is the truth?" Scotty demanded.

"Don't know that. Yet. Reckon I'll find out, though. Only I'll need some help." Keen eyes surveyed the two boys.

Rick worked his hand line absently. "You mean you want us to help?"

"Seems I've read about you boys solving a mystery or two, haven't I?"

"We've had a couple of lucky breaks," Scotty said. "We're not real detectives."

Cap'n Mike tried his line and muttered, "Feels like a cunner is stealing my bait. Well, boys, I wouldn't be surprised none if a little luck like yours is what we need. Can't pretend, though, that you might not be walking right into something you wouldn't like. Anything that scares Tom Tyler is something anyone with sense would be afraid of."

Rick hauled in his line and saw that his bait was gone. He rebaited, his mind on what he already knew of the case. "I've been wanting to ask you," he said. "That answer you gave to Jerry when he asked where Tom Tyler was. You said 'Inside. Surrounded by fools.' What did you mean?"

Cap'n Mike sniffed. "Just what I said. If the constable and the rest hadn't been fools they would have known that Tom Tyler was afraid to talk. Just like plenty of others are afraid."

Rick picked up his ears. "Others? Cap'n, I think you know a few things you haven't told us."

The old seaman hauled in his line and grunted when he saw that his bait had been stolen. "Reckon we got too many bait stealers down below now. Either of you boys hungry?"

"I am," Scotty said promptly.

"I could eat," Rick admitted. He looked at his watch. It was almost noon.

"Then let's haul anchor and get out of here."

In a moment the hand lines were wound on driers and the anchor stowed. At Cap'n Mike's direction, Rick pointed the launch to the south, toward the town. The old man took out his pocketknife, whetted it briefly on the sole of his shoe, and commenced to clean and fillet the fish they had caught. Scotty slipped into the seat beside Rick.

"What do you think about trying to solve this one?"

Rick shrugged. There was nothing he enjoyed as much as a mystery, but he wanted more information from Captain Michael O'Shannon before he agreed to anything. He had suspected that the old seaman knew more than he was saying. "We'll wait and see what develops," he said. "Okay with you?"

"Suits me," Scotty agreed.

The launch sped past Million Dollar Row, leaving behind a string of fishy waste as Cap'n Mike went on with his cleaning. By the time they were even with the town he had a handsome stack of white boneless fillets all ready for the pan. He brought them forward and took a seat next to Scotty. "Guess these'll taste mighty good. Got a little fresh bread and plenty of butter to go with 'em."

Rick pointed to a large barnlike structure on the biggest pier in front of the town. "What's that?"

"Fish market. That's where most of the trawlers load and unload. It's quiet now, because the fleet is out, but after dark when they come in, and early in the morning before they leave--that's the busiest place in these parts. I'll take you down there one of these times. Might be we'll find a couple of answers there."

27

He pointed to an old windmill on the shore just below the town. "Steer for that."

"Do you live there?" Scotty asked.

"I live in a shack behind it. But there's a place to tie up. You'll see it in a minute."

As the captain had said, there was a small dock in front of the windmill. Rick headed the launch for it and in a short time they were tied up. Behind the mill, which was an old ruin that had been used a half century before for grinding meal, was the road leading south from Seaford. Across the road was a weather-beaten fisherman's shack.

Cap'n Mike pushed the door open. "It ain't no palace," he said, "but it's home and I'm proud to welcome you. Come on in."

Inside, Rick stared around him with appreciative surprise. The little shanty was as neat and efficient as a ship's cabin. On one side was a tiny galley with everything neatly stowed. On the other was a built-in bunk. The walls had been papered with old charts, and he saw that most of them were of the New York–New Jersey area. A ship's lantern, wired for electricity, hung so low that it almost brushed Scotty's head. Ship models lined the mantel.

Cap'n Mike was already at work in the galley. With no waste motion he produced a coffeepot, filled it with water, dumped in a handful of coffee and put it on the stove. He whisked a match across the seat of his pants and lit the kerosene. Then he produced a paper bag, shook in flour, salt and pepper, dumped in the fish and closed the bag, shaking it violently a few times with one hand while he produced a frying pan with the other. In a moment the pan was full of frying fish. A breadbox yielded a loaf of homemade bread.

Before Rick and Scotty quite realized that lunch was ready, he had them seated at a table that folded down from the wall, with a smoking platter of fillets in front of them.

"Eat," he commanded.

Rick was no fish fancier, but he had to admit that this was delicious. And the coffee, in spite of the apparent carelessness with which it had been made, was the best ever.

When the last drop had been consumed, Cap'n Mike pushed back his chair. "Let's get down to brass tacks," he said. "Do you go along with me or not?"

Rick dropped into the idiom of the sea. "I like to know the course before I haul anchor."

Cap'n Mike chuckled. "Didn't expect caution or wisdom from you."

Scotty grinned. "Don't worry. He's neither cautious nor wise. He can't wait to get started and neither can I. But Rick's right. We have to know the whole story."

"Right. Well, there isn't much. Something's been going on in Seaford. Don't ask me what, because I don't know. I think Tom Tyler does, and I think his finding out is what led to the wreck of the Sea Belle." He held up his hand as Rick's lips framed a question. "You're going to ask me how I know that. Well, I don't know it. I just suspect it. I was a mite too positive when I said I knew. All I know is Tom Tyler told me one day that he had an idea that something strange was going on at the Creek House, and that he intended to find out what it was. Now! He must have had a good idea that whatever was going on was crooked, because Tom isn't the kind of man to pry into folks' business without a good purpose."

"Do you think he found out?" Rick asked.

"I do. I think he found out four nights ago. I was sitting in my dory jigging for eels a little distance down from the Creek House fence right at the mouth of Salt Creek. I saw Tom. He didn't know I saw him. He came around the corner of the fence and for a minute he was silhouetted against a light. I didn't see his face, but I'm sure. Known him since he was a shaver. Next morning I bumped into him at the pier, getting ready to go out on the Sea Belle . He said to see him at his house that night, because he had something to talk to me about. Well, I saw him that night, but not at his house. He was sitting at a corner table in Sam's Lobster House, and can you guess who was with him?"

"Red Kelso?"

Cap'n Mike nodded at Rick. "It was Kelso. He was doing the talking, too, and from the expression on Tom's face, he wasn't saying anything Tom liked a whole lot. After a while he left, and I went over to Tom. I asked casual-like what it was he wanted to talk with me about and he froze up like a clam. He was scared, at first. Then he seemed to get sort of mad, too, because he said, 'I'm going to call his bluff. Wait and see.'"

"Meaning Kelso," Scotty said.

"I reckon, but Tom wouldn't talk. He said it was better that I didn't know what he was talking about. He got up and left and I didn't see him again until last night at City Hall after he wrecked the Sea Belle."

Rick thought it over. The logical deduction was that Tom Tyler had somehow gotten suspicious of the Kelsos and what they were doing at Creek House and

29

had gone spying. Kelso had found out Tyler had spied on him and had warned him, although Rick couldn't imagine what club he had held over Tyler's head. Tyler had ignored the warning and somehow Kelso had contrived to wreck the trawler. But how?

"Was the regular crew aboard the Sea Belle?" he asked.

"Yes. Just the regulars. All good men who've sailed with Tom Tyler for more'n ten years."

"You said Mrs. Tyler was afraid, too," Scotty remembered.

Cap'n Mike shrugged. "Probably Tom talked the whole thing over with her."

There had been an air of tension at the wreck last night, Rick thought. Maybe other fishermen were in it, too. He put the question to Cap'n Mike.

"I don't think so," the old man said. "The whole town knows something's up. They know Tom Tyler doesn't wince at shadows. If he's afraid, and they know he is, he's got reasons. That makes 'em all uneasy. But there is one gang that I'm sure is mixed up in this, and that's the bunch on the Albatross. She's a fishing craft just like Tom's, only her skipper isn't much like Tom. Name's Brad Marbek."

Rick stretched his legs. "Why do you think he and his crew are mixed up in it?"

"Eel fishing is a good business for them as wants information," Cap'n Mike said.

Rick hid a smile. The old seaman was bursting with curiosity about the Creek House and its new inhabitants. He had a picture of him sitting patiently at the mouth of Salt Creek, ostensibly fishing but actually watching to see what he could find out.

"I've seen the Albatross tied up at Salt Creek pier three times," the captain went on. "Now! Why would a trawler, loaded to the gunwales with menhaden, stop at the hotel before coming in to the fish wharves to unload?"

"Not for social purposes, that's certain," Rick said.

"Find out why and we're a lot closer to the solution," Cap'n Mike stated.

Rick had the germ of an idea. "How far out do the trawlers go?"

"Few miles. Fishing grounds start a couple of miles out. Why?"

"Just an idea."

Scotty's eyes met Rick's. "Thinking about going to take a look?"

"Could be. What time do they leave here, and what time do they get back?"

"They leave about four in the morning at this time of year. Mostly they don't get back until around nine. They like to get to the grounds by daylight and fish

30

until dark. If they get a full load before dark, of course they come in earlier."

Rick grinned at Scotty. "Ever wanted to be a reporter?"

"Nope. My spelling isn't that good."

"Well, you're going to be one. Let's get home. I want to make a call to the Whiteside Morning Record ."

Cap'n Mike's eyes brightened. "So you'll work along with me, hey? Knew you would. What happens now?"

"First thing is to interview Captain Tyler and his crew," Rick said.

Cap'n Mike shook his head. "You'd be wasting time. I've already tried. Tom's not saying a word, even to his old friends, and the crew has orders from him not to talk. They're loyal. You'll get nothing out of 'em."

"All right," Rick said, disappointed. If the fishermen wouldn't talk to Cap'n Mike they certainly wouldn't talk to him and Scotty. "Then we'll go back to Spindrift and do a couple of chores. We'll come back to Seaford tonight. I'd like to get a look at the Albatross, if you can fix it."

"Easy." Cap'n Mike rubbed his hands together gleefully. "I'm betting we can get Tom Tyler out of this."

Rick scratched his head thoughtfully. "Don't get your hopes too high, Cap'n Mike. We're only a couple of amateurs, remember."

"Some amateurs are better than some professionals, no matter what the business. I'm not worried anymore."

Cap'n Mike walked down to the boat landing in front of the old windmill with them. "How will you come down tonight?"

"I'll try to borrow a car," Rick said. "Think Jerry will lend us his, Scotty?"

"If he isn't using it. If he is, maybe we can borrow Gus's."

Scotty walked to the stern of the launch and untied the line that held it to the pier. Rick loosed the bow line, then jumped into the pilot's seat. As he did so, he sat on a sheet of paper. He had left no paper on the seat. He rescued it and turned it over. There was a message on the back, printed in pencil in huge block letters. Its content sent a sudden shiver through him. He beckoned to Scotty and handed it to him. "Looks like someone can read enough to get our home port off the stern of the launch."

Scotty scanned it rapidly, then whistled softly. For Cap'n Mike's benefit, he read it aloud.

KEEP OUT OF THIS. KEEP OUT OF SEAFORD

AND STAY AWAY FROM SHANNON.
STAY AT SPINDRIFT WHERE YOU BELONG.
YOU'LL GET HURT IF YOU DON'T.

Scotty's face took on an injured expression. "To read that," he complained, "you'd think we weren't wanted here!"

Chapter 5: The Mysterious Phone Call

Rick hung up the phone in the Spindrift library and turned to Scotty. "Jerry is using his car tonight. But Duke says okay. He'll make out a reporter's identity card for you and a photographer's card for me. Only if anything interesting turns up, we have to give him a story."

"Good thing papers have rewrite men," Scotty said, grinning. "It's all I can do to write a readable letter. A news story would be way beyond me."

Rick picked up the phone again. "I'll see if Gus is using his car."

Gus, owner, chief mechanic, and general factotum of the Whiteside Airport, had loaned his car to Rick on several occasions. His hope, he explained every time, was that Rick would drive it to pieces so he could collect the insurance and get a better one.

In a moment Gus answered. "It's Gus."

"Rick here, Gus. That ancient clunk of yours still running?"

Gus's voice assumed wounded dignity. "Are you speaking of my airplane or my automobile?"

"Your limousine. Using it tonight?"

"Nope. Don't drive it any more than I have to. When do you want it?"

"About eight, if that's all right."

"Okay. I'll drop it off at the dock. Don't bother bringing it back. Just let me know where it is so I can tell the insurance company."

"I'm a safe driver, Gus," Rick said with a grin.

"If I believed that I wouldn't lend you the car. Leave it in my back yard when you get through, huh?"

"Thanks a million, Gus. I'll take good care of it."

"Don't. You'll spoil it."

Rick rang off. "What time is it?"

"About half past three," Scotty said. "Why?"

"Let's take the Cub up for a little spin."

Scotty chuckled. "You're never as happy as when you're trying to unravel a mystery. Any mystery."

"You don't like it," Rick scoffed. "You like a peaceful, quiet life, a book and a hammock. That's for you. Why don't you go get one of your Oat Operas to read and leave the mystery to me?"

"Got to keep you out of trouble," Scotty said amiably. "It isn't because I'm interested."

They walked from the house into the orchard that separated the low, gray stone laboratory buildings from the house and headed toward the air strip. The strip was grass-covered and just big enough for a small plane like Rick's. It ran along the seaward side of the island, with the orchard on one side and the sea cliff on the other.

"Just thought," Scotty said suddenly. "We'd better have some binoculars if we're going out to take a look at the fleet."

"I'll warm up while you get them," Rick agreed. He started the engine and warmed the plane until Scotty arrived with a pair of ten-power binoculars.

Scotty untied the parking ropes and pulled out the wheel chocks, then got into his seat. "Let's go," he said.

Rick nodded and advanced the throttle. In a moment the Cub lifted easily from the grass.

Rick settled down to the business of flying. He looked at the sea below and estimated the wind force. Mentally he figured his probable drift, then decided on south-southeast as his compass heading, and swung the little plane on course.

"Checked the equipment recently?" Scotty asked.

He referred to the two-man life raft and signaling pistol Rick had purchased from Navy surplus for just such overwater flights as this.

"Went through it Saturday," Rick said. "But don't worry. We won't get your feet wet."

"You hadn't better," Scotty retorted. "These are new shoes I have on." He paused. "What do you think about that warning?"

They had discussed it thoroughly on the way home from Seaford, examining all possibilities. "I haven't changed my mind," Rick said. "I think it was Carrots Kelso."

He reasoned that Red Kelso, the boy's father, had too much sense to try warning them away. The only purpose the warning would serve would be to arouse their curiosity even more--which it had certainly done.

"That Carrots is a queer one," Scotty said. He had to raise his voice slightly because of the engine's drone. "Did you notice the rifle he carried?"

"And how! It looked like a .30-30."

34

"It wasn't."

Rick looked at Scotty in surprise. "No?"

"Nope. It looked like one because of the lever. Sport carbines have those to lever cartridges into the chamber. But this one had a lever for pumping air. I've only seen one like it before, and a professional hunter in Australia had that one. He used it for collecting specimens when he didn't want to make noise. Sometimes he found several wallabies or Tasmanian wolves together and he could get two or three before they knew what was up."

"You mean an air gun has enough power to use for hunting?" Rick knew modern air guns had high penetrating power, but he had never heard of one powerful enough to use on animals as big as wolves.

"This model has," Scotty told him. "It was made by the Breda Gun Company in Czechoslovakia before the war. The slug is about .25 caliber, but heavier than the kind we have in America."

"Wonder where he got it," Rick mused.

"Hard to tell. They're expensive guns, believe me."

The Cub had been flying only a few hundred feet above the water. Behind them, the New Jersey coast was still in sight. Rick climbed to a thousand feet and told Scotty to start looking for the fishing fleet.

"How many shots can you get out of that air rifle?" Rick asked.

"Just one. It's automatic loading, but it has to be pumped up each time. That's not as hard as it sounds, though, because the pump is made so that two strokes will give it a full air charge. It's about as fast firing as a single-shot .22 rifle."

Rick's eyes scanned the horizon. "How do you suppose Carrots tracked us to Cap'n Mike's shack?"

"Easy enough. He could hike along the shore and keep us in sight."

"He was risking being seen when he put that warning on the seat. Suppose one of us had looked out the window?"

"Then he would have pretended to be just hiking, or looking at the boat or something. It wasn't really much of a risk."

"I suppose not," Rick agreed. Small specks on the horizon caught his eye suddenly and he pointed. "There's the fleet!"

Scotty held the binoculars to his eyes. "Sure enough. About eight trawlers so far, pretty well scattered."

In a few moments they could see clouds of gulls and petrels around the boats, a sure sign of plenty of fish. Then they made out the details of the big nets used

35

by the fishermen for catching the menhaden.

"See if you can spot the Albatross," Rick said.

"You'll have to go down and pass each boat, then. I couldn't make out the names from this height."

"Okay. Here we go."

On each of the craft, fishermen waved as the Cub sped past. Scotty read the names aloud. None of the trawlers was the Albatross.

Rick put the Cub into a climb. "There must be other trawlers around. Let's go up and take a look."

Scotty shook his head. "I have a better idea. We'll see the Albatross tonight, anyway. Why not go into shore and fly over Creek House? Sometimes you can see things from the air you can't see from the ground."

Rick considered. Flying out to the fleet had been only an impulse anyway; he hadn't expected to see anything. He was quite sure the Albatross would look and act just like the rest of the Seaford fleet.

"Good idea," he said finally, and banked the Cub around. He pointed the little plane south of west to compensate for the wind, then settled back.

Rick kept an eye out for landmarks as the coast approached and presently he made out the steel towers of an antenna field. That would be the Loran radio range south of Seaford. He had compensated a little too much for drift. He banked north and in a few moments Scotty spotted Seaford.

Rick dropped down, but kept out to sea so that he wouldn't violate the law about flying too low over towns. He saw the windmill and Cap'n Mike's shack behind it.

"Go past Smugglers' Reef and then turn and come back over Creek House," Scotty suggested.

Rick nodded. Dead ahead he could see the curving arm of the reef and the wreck of Tyler's trawler. He saw that the fishing craft had piled up just about midway between the navigation light on the reef's tip and the old tower where the light formerly had been. Men were working about the trawler. Then, as the Cub flashed overhead, he saw a large truck that had backed down the reef toward the wreck as far as it was safe to go.

Scotty had been watching through the glasses. As Rick swung wide out to sea and banked around to go south again, he said, "Know what they're doing down there? They're stripping the wreck."

"That makes sense," Rick said. "Probably the insurance company wants to salvage what it can. They'd have to act fast before sea water ruined the engines."

He banked sharply over Brendan's Marsh. To the right was the highway leading from Whiteside to Seaford. Between the highway and the sea was the marsh. Although the marsh looked like solid growth from the ground, it could be seen that it was cut up by narrow waterways, most of which wandered aimlessly through the rushes and then vanished. Salt Creek was sharply defined, however, indicating that it was much deeper than the surrounding water.

The Creek House was fenced in on only two sides, he saw. The high boards separated it from the next hotel on the south, and from the road on the sea front. But inland, a continuation of the marsh served as a dividing line. Salt Creek made the fourth side. The old mansion was set in the middle of the square with a big combination garage and boathouse behind it, almost against the marsh on the creek side. The doors were open and he could make out a black car, probably a coupe or two-door model, in one of the stalls.

"See anyone?" Scotty asked.

"Not a soul." Evidently the Kelsos were indoors.

Rick climbed as the Cub passed over Seaford, then turned out to sea and went northward again. Scotty kept the glasses on Smugglers' Reef. As they flashed past, he swiveled sharply. "Rick, make another run, right over the wreck."

"You won't be able to see it if I go right over it," Rick objected.

"I don't want to see the wreck, I want a closer look at the old tower."

Rick shot a glance at his pal. "See something?"

"I'm not sure."

"I'll throttle down so you can get a better look." He made a slow bank, lined up the wreck and throttled down, dropping the nose to a shallow glide in order to maintain flying speed. As the Cub passed the old tower, he looked curiously. He couldn't imagine what had attracted Scotty's interest. The thing was only a steel framework, red with rust. Not even the top platform was left.

Off Seaford, he banked out to sea again.

"See enough?"

Scotty dropped the binoculars to his lap. "I saw bright metal on the lowest cross girder. I couldn't tell much, but it looked like a deep scratch. And some of the rust had been flaked off around the spot, too. I could tell because it was a redder color than the rest."

Rick thought it over. "I can't make anything out of that," he said finally. "What's your guess?"

37

Scotty shrugged. "I don't have one. But it's a cinch someone has been up there, and within the past couple of days, too. Raw metal rusts fast right over the sea like that, and this spot was bright enough to attract my attention. Maybe we'd better have a closer look from the ground."

"It wouldn't hurt," Rick agreed. "Well, what now?"

"Might as well go home," Scotty said. "We can take it easy until after dinner, and then go to Whiteside, pick up those cards from Duke and get the car from Gus."

They had been flying steadily north. A moment later Spindrift loomed on the horizon. Rick saw the gray lab building and, to its left, Pirate's Field where the rocket launcher had once stood. He waited until the Cub was abreast of the old oak on the mainland that he used as a landmark, then cut the throttle. The plane lost altitude rapidly, passed a few feet over the radar antenna on the lab building and settled to the grass strip. Rick gunned the tail around and rolled to the parking place.

They staked down the Cub and walked through the orchard to the house. In the kitchen, Mrs. Brant was rolling out piecrust. She smiled at the boys. "Been riding?"

"We went out to watch the fishing fleet," Rick said, "then swung down over Seaford for another look at that wrecked trawler. What kind of pie, Mom?"

"Butterscotch."

Scotty smacked his lips. "We should have waited a little while, then we could have had a sample when we got in."

"No samples," Mrs. Brant said. "It would spoil your supper."

"Not mine," Scotty replied. "Nothing spoils my supper. Got any doughnuts handy, Mom?"

Mrs. Brant sighed. "In the stone crock. And there's milk in the refrigerator. But only one doughnut!"

"Only one," Scotty agreed. "How about you, Rick?"

"I'm not hungry. I think I'll go up and work on the camera for a while." He would have over an hour to work on it before it was time to eat. He started for the stairs, then paused as the telephone rang.

Hartson Brant, who was working in the library, answered it and called, "Rick? It's for you."

"I'll take it upstairs, Dad." He hurried to the top of the stairs and picked up the hall phone.

"Hello?"

"Rick Brant?"

Rick stiffened. It was a man's voice, but obviously disguised as though the man spoke through a handkerchief held over the mouthpiece.

"Yes. Who is it?"

"A friend," the disguised voice answered. "You're a nice kid and I don't like to see you getting into trouble. Keep out of Seaford. Remember that! Keep out of Seaford and stop flying over in your airplane or you're going to get hurt. You won't be warned again. Next time, you'll wake up in a hospital!"

There was a click as the speaker hung up.

Chapter 6: The "Albatross"

"Know what I like about you?" Scotty said.

"My charm," Rick answered. "Or is it that I like food as much as you do?"

"Neither. What I like about you is your caution. The very soul of prudence, that's what you are. Your instinct for self-preservation is exceeded by only one thing."

"My," Rick said. "That's almost poetic. What's the one thing?"

"Your instinct for getting into trouble," Scotty stated. "You get a warning to stay away from Seaford, so what happens next?" He waved at the scenery as they sped past in Gus's old car. "Naturally we head for Seaford at ninety miles an hour, not even stopping to pick up our press cards."

Rick laughed. "Be accurate. This old heap can't go ninety miles an hour. Besides, it's only my never-ending search for the truth that leads me to Seaford. I want to find out if the warning is true."

Scotty sighed. "Whoever it was that phoned should know you as I do. If we needed anything to sharpen the famous Brant nose for trouble, it was that phone call. I suppose now we'll spend all our waking hours commuting back and forth to Seaford."

"Not all," Rick corrected. "Some of the time we'll be in Seaford."

"Any idea who it was that phoned?"

"It could have been anyone. But I don't think it was Carrots Kelso. The voice was an older man's. Maybe it was his father, but I didn't hear enough of his voice to recognize it."

"Why should anyone worry about us looking into things?"

"Respect," Rick said, wincing as the car bounced across Salt Creek Bridge. "Respect for the genius of Spindrift's two leading detectives. Can't think of any other reason."

"Unless whatever is going on would be so obvious to anyone who took the trouble to investigate that the party concerned doesn't even want two simple-minded souls like us poking around."

"Such modesty," Rick clucked.

"Okay, Hawkshaw," Scotty said resignedly. "On to Seaford. We'll probably find the answer just as the villain lowers the boom on us."

Rick swung into the Seaford turnoff and slowed for the main street. He went straight ahead to the water front and then turned right. In a few moments the car drew up in front of Cap'n Mike's shack.

The captain opened the door and peered out. "Be with you in a minute." In much less than a minute he was out again, clad in a jacket and officer's cap.

"Howdy," he greeted them. "See much from your airplane?"

"How did you know it was our airplane?" Rick asked curiously.

"Pshaw! You don't give people credit for knowing much, do you? I'll bet everyone in Seaford knows about your airplane: Everyone who reads the Whiteside Morning Record, anyway."

"But all Cubs look alike," Rick protested, "and most of them are painted yellow."

Cap'n Mike snorted. "What of it? No other yellow planes in this area, and you been seen on the ground in Seaford twice already. What would anyone think? Especially when you're on a direct bearing for Spindrift when you leave?"

"He's got something there," Scotty said. "It's a logical conclusion."

Rick had to agree. "Well, you're the guide, Cap'n, where to?"

"The pier." Cap'n Mike looked at the fast-fading light in the west. "It's time for the trawlers to be coming in. Reckon we'll talk to a couple of folks and get a look at the Albatross and her crew."

Rick turned the car around and headed for town. "Why don't you tell us all you know about the Albatross visiting Creek House?"

"I intended to. First off, the Albatross has been there three times that I know of. And each time she has put in on her way back from the fishing grounds. Now, that's mighty strange. First thing a captain thinks of is getting his fish into port. But not Brad Marbek. Instead, he lays at the Creek House pier until nigh onto midnight. Then he puts into the wharf and unloads his fish. What do you make out of that?"

Rick could make nothing out of it. The Albatross certainly wouldn't be calling at Creek House just to be sociable. "Were these calls made at regular intervals?" he asked.

"Nope. One was two weeks ago, one was four nights ago, and the last time was night before last."

"Wasn't four nights ago the night you saw Tom Tyler at Creek House?" Scotty recalled.

"It was. That's one reason why I'm sure the Albatross is tied up with the wreck of the Sea Belle."

Rick searched for possible reasons why the trawler should tie up at Creek House and rejected all but one. He had the beginnings of an idea, but he needed to think about it a little more before he broached it.

"Cap'n, you've been keeping an eye on the Kelsos for quite a while, sounds like," Rick said. "Do they ever have any visitors?"

"Haven't seen any."

"No trucks?" Rick asked.

"Haven't seen any."

They were approaching the big, shedlike fish pier. It was brilliantly lighted. At Cap'n Mike's direction, Rick pulled off the street and parked.

"What happens to the menhaden after they're unloaded?" Scotty wanted to know.

"Ever notice that one-story building next to the pier? Well, they go into that on conveyer belts. Then the oil is cooked out of them and what's left is turned into feed or fertilizer. You'd know if you'd ever been here while the plant was processing and the wind was inshore. Dangdest smell you ever smelled; Like to ruin your nose."

Rick sniffed the fishy air. "I believe it," he said.

Cap'n Mike had been leading the way toward the big pier. Now he turned onto the pier itself. Some trawlers already were tied up and were being unloaded by bucket cranes. The reek of fish was strong enough to make Rick wish for a gas mask. He saw Scotty's nose wrinkle and knew his pal wasn't enjoying it, either.

The captain stopped at the first trawler and hailed the bridge. A big man in an officer's cap answered the hail.

"Let's go aboard," Cap'n Mike said. "This here is the Jennie Lake. We'll talk with Bill Lake for a minute."

Bill Lake was the skipper, and the man they had seen directing the unloading from the bridge. He greeted Cap'n Mike cordially. The captain introduced the two boys and Lake shook hands without taking his eyes from the unloading operation. Rick saw a scoop drop into the hold and come up with a slippery half-ton of menhaden. Then it sped along a beam track into the big shed, paused over a wide conveyer belt, lowered to within a few feet of the belt and dumped its load. A clerk just inside the door marked the load on a board. Rick looked for the winch operator and found him opposite the clerk.

The scoop came back rapidly, sped out the track extension above the hold, and paused. Bill Lake signaled and the big bucket dropped slowly. At a further signal, it opened its jaws and plunged into the mass of fish, then slowly crunched closed and lifted again. There was certainly no waste motion here, Rick thought.

Cap'n Mike asked, too casually, "What'd you think of Tom Tyler running on Smugglers' Reef, Bill?"

Bill's cordiality seemed to freeze up. "None of my business," he said shortly. "Can't pass judgment on a fellow skipper."

Cap'n Mike nodded. "Reckon that's right. Bill, how did you find visibility last night?"

"None too good. There was a heavy current running, too."

"That's interesting. How'd you know that?"

"Patch of mist drifted in. Anyway, I lost the light for a bit. When the mist cleared, the current had set us two points off course." Captain Lake's forehead wrinkled as he watched the scoop return for another load. "Mighty funny, too. Usually there's no current to speak of off Brendan's Marsh. But I've said for quite a while that the currents hereabouts are changing and it looks like this proves it."

"Was Captain Tyler directly ahead of you, sir?" Rick asked.

"Not directly. He was three ahead, the way I figure. Brad Marbek was right behind him, then came Jim Killian."

"How far apart were you?" Rick inquired.

"Quite a ways. Jim was pretty close in front of me, but Brad was almost out of my sight. Don't know how close he followed Tom."

Cap'n Mike spat over the side. "Sad business, anyway," he said. "Well, Bill, I'm taking these lads on a little tour of the pier. Reckon we'll be pushing along. Looks like you'll be busy unloading for an hour or so."

The boys shook hands with Captain Lake again, then followed their guide to the pier once more. Cap'n Mike waited until a scoopful of menhaden had passed overhead then led the way down the pier.

"I wonder if Captain Killian got set off course by that current," Rick mused. "I'd like to talk to him."

Cap'n Mike shot a glance at him. "Might be interesting at that, you thinking the same as I am?"

"We all are," Scotty replied. "That business about losing the light and having the current set him off course sounded kind of strange."

"Is he a good guy?" Rick queried.

43

"Best there is. If he says it, it happened. But it's mighty funny just the same. Reckon we'll have to find Jim Killian."

They passed three trawlers, all unloading, and Rick recognized names that Scotty had read aloud during their brief flight over the fleet. Many of the men they passed hailed Cap'n Mike. Evidently he was well known to the fisherman and pier workers.

Suddenly the old man stopped. "There's Brad Marbek's craft."

The next trawler in line was the Albatross.

Rick looked it over critically. It was indistinguishable from the others. There was the same cabin, set well forward, the same large working space aft, the same net booms. It was no dirtier nor cleaner than the others. Evidently it was filled with fish, because only the top Plimsoll number was showing. But the skipper was far from average. Brad Marbek, as Rick saw him on the deck overhead, was a bull of a man. He was about six feet tall, but his width made him look shorter. His shoulder span would have done credit to a Percheron horse, and from his shoulders his torso dropped in almost a straight line. His waist lacked only an inch or two of being as wide as his shoulders. His legs were short and thick and planted wide on the deck. His head was massive and set squarely on his shoulders with hardly any neck. He was hatless and his coarse black hair, cropped short, stood straight up like a vegetable brush. His face was weathered to a dark mahogany color.

"Not very pretty, is he?" Scotty whispered.

That, Rick thought, was a masterpiece of understatement. He started to tell Scotty that compared with Brad Marbek a Hereford bull was downright winsome, but at that moment Cap'n Mike hailed the Albatross.

"Howdy, Brad. How's fish?"

The skipper's reply was cordial enough. "Howdy, Cap'n Mike. Took another good haul today. Just startin' to unload." Marbek's black eyes surveyed the two boys briefly, then evidently dismissed them as of no importance. "Come on aboard."

"Thanks. We will." Cap'n Mike motioned to the two boys and led the way up the gangplank just as a scoop full of menhaden rose from the hold and passed overhead.

On deck, the captain introduced the boys to Marbek. Rick found his hand imprisoned in a horny mass that appeared to be controlled by steel cables instead of tendons. He tried not to wince.

44

"Best season I've seen in years," Marbek told Cap'n Mike. His voice was ridiculously high and soft, out of keeping with his physique.

"That's what everyone's saying," Cap'n Mike acknowledged. "Why, only two days ago, I heard ..."

Scotty nudged Rick with a sharp elbow. He was looking at the pier. Rick turned and followed his pal's glance, then as he saw what Scotty was looking at, he inhaled sharply. Carrots Kelso was leaning against a pillar, watching them.

"Wonder what's on his mind?" Rick asked.

Brad Marbek saw the direction of their glance. "You kids know Jimmy? He's my nephew."

The pause before Cap'n Mike spoke was proof of his surprise. "You don't say!" He changed the subject abruptly. "Say, Brad, I've been meaning to ask you. Did you notice any peculiar current offshore last night?"

"Current? Can't say I did. Why?"

"Bill Lake claims a strong current set him off course just as he picked up Smugglers' Light, about the time Tom Tyler ran aground."

Rick thought that Brad Marbek hesitated slightly and searched for the right answer.

"Now that you mention it, I did notice a little shift." A scoop whirred out of the hold, crossed the pier, dumped its load and started the return. "Let me know if you find out any more about it," Marbek said. "Right now I guess I better attend to my unloadin'."

"Sure, Brad," Cap'n Mike said. "We'll be getting on. By the way, happen to know where Jim Killian is tied up?"

"I think he's on the other side of the pier. Cross over and duck under the belts. He should be right abeam of us."

"Thanks. Let's go, boys."

Cap'n Mike led the way down the gangplank with Rick and Scotty following. Rick felt Brad Marbek's eyes on them. He had sensed tension under the fisherman's surface cordiality, and he was interested in the quick way Marbek had remembered the strange current when Cap'n Mike quoted Bill Lake.

At the foot of the gangplank, Cap'n Mike paused. "Let's find Jim. I'm getting real curious about that current Bill mentioned. What say?"

"We're right with you," Scotty replied.

Rick watched the big scoop vanish into the Albatross' hold, then looked for Carrots Kelso. He was no longer in sight. "Wonder where Carrots went to?" he

45

said to Scotty.

"Probably running to tell his father we're prowling around the pier."

Cap'n Mike led the way into the pier shed. He turned to look over his shoulder at the boys. "What'd you think of Marbek claiming young Kelso as a nephew?"

"Don't you think he really is?" Rick asked. He had to raise his voice above the noise of the scoop as it lifted from the trawler's hold.

"Surprise to me. I've known Marbek fifteen years and never heard of any family. Why--"

"Look out!"

On the heels of Scotty's cry, Rick caught a glimpse of his pal hurling Cap'n Mike headlong. He jumped forward, glancing up, just as the great fish scoop opened over his head. He put all of his energy in a forward leap to safety, but too late!

Cascading thousands of menhaden crushed him violently to the floor.

Chapter 7: Search for a Clue

As Rick fell to the floor, he twisted sideways and managed to bring up one arm to protect his head. In an instant he was buried in a great, heavy, slippery mass of fish. His nostrils filled with the oily stench, and when he opened his mouth to breathe, he closed it again on a fish tail. He spat it out, and then, furious, he struggled against the slimy weight, got his hands and feet under him and heaved. Fish cascaded from his arched back and he broke clear just as Scotty reached for him.

"You all right?" Scotty gasped.

"Yes."

Cap'n Mike, hurled clear by Scotty's rush, was getting to his feet.

Scotty departed on a dead run.

Rick collected his thoughts and yelled, "Hey! Wait! Where're you going?"

"After Kelso," Scotty called back over his shoulder.

Rick didn't know what had happened, but evidently Scotty did and was doing something about it. He ran after his friend, brushing off dirt from his clothes as he did so. He heard Cap'n Mike call, "Wait for me!" but he didn't pause.

At the entrance to the pier, Rick caught up with Scotty who was looking up and down the street, his face flushed with anger.

"He's gone. No use looking for him because he could hide anywhere around here. But we'll catch up with him one of these days, and when we do ..."

"What's it all about?" Rick demanded.

"Carrots tripped that scoop on us. I don't know how, but I know he did it."

Cap'n Mike came up behind them in time to hear Scotty. "He's the one, all right. There's an emergency trip on those scoops, set in the wall. It's in case the operator loses control. Then the scoop can be dumped without having all that weight smash against the end of the track and break things. Young Kelso must have punched the trip."

"He sure did." Rick sniffed angrily. "And I smell like ten days in a bait pail. Scotty, we've got to get home and get out of these clothes. I can't stand myself."

"Check," Scotty replied. "Well, I guess that wraps up the investigation for the night, Cap'n."

Cap'n Mike nodded. "I want to be around when you boys meet up with young Kelso. That was as fishy a trick as I ever saw pulled."

Rick looked at the old sea captain suspiciously. Cap'n Mike was having a hard time to keep from laughing. Then Rick had to grin himself. "Don't laugh too loud," he reminded. "If Scotty hadn't pushed you, you'd be smelling like a week-old herring yourself."

"I know," Cap'n Mike said. "Thanks." He threw back his head and roared.

Rick laughed, too, but when Cap'n Mike doubled up with mirth, he began to grow a little irritated. "It isn't that funny," he said, a little tartly.

Scotty chuckled. "Maybe this is what amuses him." He reached over and plucked a small menhaden from the breast pocket of Rick's jacket.

"Dangdest place to carry fresh fish I ever saw," Cap'n Mike said, and went off into gales of laughter again.

Rick took out his handkerchief and mopped his face. "Well," he said, grinning, "I'm sure glad those menhaden weren't whales."

They drove home to Whiteside with all windows wide open and newspapers on the seat to protect the car, but even so, the stench of oily fish made Rick feel a little queasy.

"We can't go to Spindrift like this," he complained. "Tell you what, I'll take the wood road that goes down by the tidal flats. Then one of us can cross over, get clean clothes for both of us and some soap and towels. We can go to Walton's Pond, take a swim, scrub off the fish, and change."

"Good idea," Scotty agreed. "But these coats and pants will have to be dry cleaned."

"That's easy. There's a night service door at the cleaners where we can just push them through."

Scotty chuckled. "You won't get any thanks for that. The whole dry cleaning place will smell like a fish market before morning."

"We'll wrap them up good in plenty of newspapers."

"Where do we get the papers?"

"From the Morning Record. I want to go there, anyway."

Scotty gave him a sideways glance. "Got an idea?"

"Just a glimmer." Rick's lips tightened. "And I'll tell you something else. Until now, this case was just sort of interesting for itself, but now I have a personal interest. I think the Kelsos are at the bottom of it."

"And we owe them a debt," Scotty finished. "Carrots, anyway. What do you suppose he dumped the scoop on us for?"

Rick shrugged. "Sheer poison meanness. And weren't we warned not to go to Seaford?"

An hour later, when they had cleaned up, the boys returned the car to Gus, apologized for the faint but definite aroma of dead menhaden, and walked to the Morning Record office.

Duke Barrows, a veteran newspaperman but young in years, greeted them cordially. "Hello, Rick, Scotty. Here are those cards you asked for." He swiveled his chair around and regarded them with interested eyes. "Getting anywhere on that Seaford yarn?"

"We're still feeling around," Rick replied. "But there's a good story in it if we can find the lead."

"Keep working then," Duke said. "I'll pay you space rates if it hits page one."

"How much is that?" Scotty wanted to know.

"Twenty-five cents a column inch on this sheet. You didn't expect to get rich, did you?"

Rick returned Duke's grin. "If this story is as good as I think it is, we'll just about get rich. You'll want to cover the whole front page with it."

"Can't be that good," Duke returned.

Rick looked around the office. "Where's Jerry?"

"In the composing room. He'll be back in a minute. Got anything on your mind?"

"Just an idea. Do you keep a file of New York papers?"

"Over there. On the shelf. Help yourself."

Rick nodded his thanks. "Let's go give my idea a try, Scotty."

Scotty tucked his press card into his wallet. "I could probably help if I knew what the idea was."

Rick explained briefly. He wanted to check the shipping sections for the dates when the Albatross had been seen at Creek House. He particularly wanted to know what ships had arrived at New York at noon or before on those dates. He was interested in ships arriving from southern ports in the Caribbean, or from southern Europe. That, he figured, would give them only the ships that might have been standing off Seaford in the early hours before dawn on the critical dates. He had a vague idea that he might find some sort of similarity in the ships that had been off Seaford on the critical dates. The registry might be the same, or the ownership.

But when the compilation was complete, there were no similarities at all. In fact, so far as he could determine, no ship had been off Seaford during the time he had chosen as having the best possibilities.

As they walked toward the Whiteside boat landing after saying good night to Duke and Jerry, Rick rapidly reviewed all they knew about the wreck of Tom Tyler's trawler and the events at Seaford.

"I sure thought I had the connecting link," he said. "I still think so, even if there wasn't any evidence in the papers. It's the only answer that makes any sense."

Scotty nodded. "Keep talking."

"Okay. The Kelsos suddenly arrive at Seaford and move into Creek House. Then the Albatross starts making visits at a time when no fisherman in his right mind would pay calls. So Brad Marbek must be going to Creek House on his way back from the fishing grounds for a good business reason. Right?"

"It figures. Go ahead."

"Tom Tyler spied on Creek House, and he found out something. Red Kelso warned him, and Tyler refused to take the warning. Result: his ship was wrecked. We don't know how yet, but we'll find out. Another thing: Mrs. Tyler was frightened, and Tom Tyler is afraid to talk. What's your guess on that?"

Scotty kicked a pebble out of the path. "Kelso again. When Tyler didn't take the first warning, his trawler was wrecked and he was told that next time something would happen to his family. That's the only threat they could make stick with a man like Tyler. If they threatened him, he'd laugh at them. But if they threatened his wife and little girl ..."

"That's the way I see it, too. Now, what kind of business requires a boat, a house on a secluded part of the beach, and a guard with a rifle?"

"Smuggling," Scotty said flatly.

Smuggling. It was the answer that fitted. Rick didn't know yet what kind of smuggling, but he intended to find out. "If you were the Kelsos, and if you were bringing contraband into Creek House, how would you get it out of Seaford?" he asked.

Scotty thought it over. "Not trucks," he said. "Cap'n Mike said he hadn't seen any trucks calling at Creek House. How about taking it somewhere in a small boat?"

In his mind's eye Rick saw the countryside surrounding Creek House as he had seen it from the air. "Right up Salt Creek," he said excitedly. "How about that? If they unloaded at the pier when the Albatross came in and then reloaded into a motor dory or some other kind of small boat, they could take it right up Salt Creek to the bridge. Then all they would need would be a truck waiting there. And if they did it late at night, there wouldn't be any traffic to worry about."

"That must be it!" Scotty exclaimed. Then he sobered. "But how are we going to find out if that's the answer?"

There was only one way. "I guess we're just going to have to see for ourselves," Rick said. As they passed the dry cleaning establishment, he took the bundle of newspaper-wrapped clothes he had been carrying and dropped them into the night-service opening. A whiff of departed menhaden smote his nose forcefully and he added grimly, "Believe me, it'll be a pleasure!"

Chapter 8: The Old Tower

Rick tightened the last screw that held the searchlight-telescope unit to his camera and looked at it with satisfaction. "I should get a picture," he murmured. There were still quite a few unknown factors. He knew the theoretical power of the infrared searchlight, but only an actual test would tell whether it gave enough light for the rather slow infrared film emulsion. He was sure that it wouldn't give enough light at its extreme range of eight hundred yards. In all probability, he would not get an image on the film at a distance greater than two hundred.

It was a little strange to think in terms of light. True, infrared was light. But it was not visible to the human eye. The searchlight would cast no beam that could be seen, although anyone close to it would be able to see dimly the hot filament of the bulb.

Another unknown was the ability of the film emulsion to register the reflected infrared rays of his particular searchlight. The emulsion had been designed originally for infrared flash bulbs. The motion-picture film had been made at his special order. It was not a stock item. He wished Professor Gordon were at Spindrift. Gordon could have measured the wave length of the searchlight on the lab equipment. Rick wasn't skilled enough to use the delicate spectroscopic wave analyzer as yet and Hartson Brant was busy with a problem in the library and couldn't be disturbed. He hoped he would have a chance to ask his father before he tested the camera.

He rechecked the data that had come with the film and started to do some figuring.

Scotty came in just as the phone rang downstairs. Both boys waited expectantly, and in a moment Mrs. Brant called. "It's an out-of-town call, for either one of you."

"We'll take it up here, Mom," Rick called back. He and Scotty raced for the landing.

Scotty reached the phone first. "Hello?" He nodded at Rick. "It's Cap'n Mike."

Something had told Rick that the call would have to do with the Seaford case. He glanced at his watch. It was almost noon.

Scotty held his hand over the mouthpiece. "He wants to know if we're coming down today; says he has something to talk over with us."

Rick said quickly, "We'll be down by boat right after lunch."

Scotty relayed the information and hung up. "He didn't say what it was, but he sounded worried. Wanted to know why we didn't come down this morning."

"Afraid of getting smacked with a fresh tuna." Rick grinned. "By the way, did you call Jerry while I was working on the camera?"

"I sure did. He got all excited. I had to calm him down a little before he went and looked up the answer."

Scotty had phoned at Rick's suggestion to find out from Jerry's newspaper sources what action to take in case they found evidence of smuggling at Seaford.

"He said to report it to the nearest Federal authorities, either the Coast Guard or FBI in this area. But he said to be sure we had something more than suspicion to go on."

"A good idea," Rick agreed. "It wouldn't do to get the government all steamed up over nothing. Besides, unless we could prove it, we'd be laying ourselves open to a charge of slander. Well, let's go see if Mom can scrape up a sandwich, and then get going for Seaford."

It was not yet two o'clock when Cap'n Mike greeted the boys as they tied up at the old windmill pier. "Mighty glad you're here. Boys, we've got to really buckle down to business."

"What happened?" Rick asked. He and Scotty fell in step with the old captain and walked toward his shack.

"Tom Tyler's hearing has been set for Saturday morning."

Scotty frowned. "Today is Wednesday. That doesn't give us much time."

"I know it don't. But unless we find some answers right fast, Tom will lose his license sure as shooting. And that's not all. He'll find himself charged by the insurance company with deliberately running the Sea Belle on the reef."

Rick found a comfortable seat in the captain's shack and stretched out his legs. "Let's hold a council of war. If we're going to do anything, we'd better have a plan of action." He told Cap'n Mike of their suspicion that the Kelsos and Brad Marbek might be engaged in smuggling and waited for the old man's reaction.

Cap'n Mike rubbed his chin reflectively. "Now! It could be that you boys have something there. It could just be!"

"But what would they be smuggling?" Scotty demanded.

"Shucks. I could make you a list a mile long. Most people think it's only worthwhile to smuggle things like drugs or aliens, but I tell you many a tidy sum has been made by smuggling things just to escape paying duty on them."

"Suppose they are smuggling," Rick pointed out. "How do we prove it?"

"Catch 'em red-handed," Scotty said. "Red-handed instead of redheaded."

Rick and Cap'n Mike groaned in unison.

It was the decision they had reached the night before, and Rick had given some thought to it before going to sleep. "There are a couple of ways we might do that," he said. "First of all, we know they have to get rid of the stuff somehow. We could keep watch on Creek House until it's moved. The only trouble is, they may be letting it pile up in the hotel. That would mean sticking on the job all day and all night."

"Not practical," Scotty objected. "Mom would object to our staying out all night for maybe a week. Besides, we want to find the answer before the hearing Saturday morning."

"Then how about this," Rick continued. "We move in on them when the Albatross pulls up at Creek House to unload."

Scotty stretched out on Cap'n Mike's bed. "That's fine. But how do we know when the Albatross is going to visit the Kelsos?"

"Cap'n Mike tells us. Cap'n, according to what you said when we were here before, the Albatross sometimes stays at Creek House until almost midnight. That means that it takes them awhile to unload whatever they're smuggling."

Scotty had an objection. "If they were doing any unloading, wouldn't you have seen them, Cap'n Mike?"

The old seaman shook his head. "Nope. I didn't dare get close enough to see what was going on. Besides, my eyes ain't what they were at night. I just sat off the end of Salt Creek, letting the reeds hide me, and saw what I could, which wasn't much. If I'd gone up the creek any distance, they'd have spotted me against the sea."

Rick finished, "So you see, if Cap'n Mike could keep an eye on the creek, he'd know when the Albatross arrived. If he phoned us right away, we could be here within an hour, or even a half-hour, if we took the fast boat."

"Sounds sensible," Scotty admitted. "Any other plans?"

"Just one, which isn't very practical. We could get someone to fly out over the fleet during the most likely hours and wait for the Albatross to make contact with the supply ship. I wish we could fly at night, but we can't. The contact has to be during the darkness, and I think before dawn is the best time. If Brad Marbek made contact after he got through fishing, some of the other trawlers might see the ship coming. Then they might get curious and hang around to see why Brad was hanging back. Maybe that's what Tom Tyler did."

"But if he left and made contact before dawn, the others might think nothing of it. I don't suppose they all leave at once, do they?" Scotty asked the captain.

"Nope. They don't all leave at once, but they usually come back at the same time. And Brad has been coming back as far as Salt Creek with the rest. So I guess Rick guessed right."

Cap'n Mike did some figuring. "Tell you what. I can sit on the beach at the edge of town with a pair of night glasses. I'll borrow some. I can tell if a ship turns up Salt Creek by its running lights. Afterwards, I'll have to go a block and use the phone at Fetty's Drug Store. We'll start tonight."

Scotty got up and yawned. "That's settled. Now I'd like to look into something. We can't overlook any possible lead. Rick, remember the tower?"

"Yes." Rick got to his feet, too. "And I remember something else. That business about the shifting current and the light. Cap'n, have you talked to Captain Killian?"

"Not yet, but I surely will today. That may be worth something." He walked with them toward the pier. "But what's this tower business?"

Rick explained briefly. "We'll stop there on the way back to Spindrift."

"Phone us if Captain Killian has anything interesting to say," Scotty requested.

"I will. Now you boys be careful. Keep a weather eye out, and don't forget those warnings."

"We're not likely to," Rick assured him.

As they sped past the Seaford water front toward Smugglers' Reef, Rick plotted a plan of action. First, if they were to spy on Creek House, they needed to know a little more about the area. He assumed that they would hurry from Spindrift by boat, since it would take too long to go to Whiteside and try to get a car. The Cub was out; there was no place to land at Seaford.

The best way of finding a good hide-out from which to watch the Kelsos would be to take a photograph from the air. He could do that this very afternoon and develop it at home. An enlargement, which the photo lab at Spindrift was equipped to make, would be better than a map.

He felt better now that they had an objective. But! "Suppose the Albatross doesn't do any smuggling before Saturday?" he asked Scotty.

"Tough luck. Captain Tyler will just have to suffer a while longer. Besides, this is only a hearing. If he's tried, it won't be until later."

"Guess that's right," Rick agreed. He swung the launch around the tip of Smugglers' Reef, past the light and the wreck of the Sea Belle. For the first time since the fatal night, there was no one at the trawler or on the reef. He put the launch close in shore at the sandy strip near the Creek House fence, and Scotty jumped to the beach with the anchor as before.

Rick joined him on the sand. "Now for a look at the tower. Where did you see the marks?"

Scotty pointed to the rusted structure. There were four upright girders slanting inward from the base to where the top platform had been. Horizontal girders held the structure together one-third and two-thirds of the way up. "The marks are on the first row of cross-pieces," he said. "On this side."

The steel climbing ladder was on the Seaford, or opposite side, of the tower halfway between the uprights. Rick looked at it dubiously. "It's pretty rusty. Think it will bear our weight?"

"Maybe only one of us had better go," Scotty conceded. "I'll try it."

Rick looked at his friend's solid frame and shook his head. "I'm the lightest. I'd better do it."

"You're not that much lighter," Scotty objected. "Tell you what, let's flip for it."

"Okay." Rick produced a coin, tossed it in the air, and called, "Tails."

It was. Scotty picked up the coin and turned it over, as though making sure it wasn't tails on both sides, then handed it to Rick with a grin. "Can you always call your shots like that?"

"Only on Wednesdays." He gestured toward the high board fence that cut them off from Creek House. "Look, just to be on the safe side, you keep an eye open for the Kelsos. If you see them coming, give me a yell. I don't think they'd dare try anything in broad daylight, but you can never tell."

"All right. I'll stick near the boat."

As Scotty walked back to the launch, Rick went to the base of the tower and looked up. The frame seemed secure enough in spite of the rust. He jumped for the first rung of the ladder and hauled himself up. In a moment he was on the horizontal girder. The scratches Scotty had seen from the air were clearly visible. To reach them, he had to work around the girders to the opposite side. He stood up and found his balance, then walked easily to the corner girder, rounded it and crossed to the other side. The marks were only a few feet away.

56

The upper stories of Creek House were on and above his level now. He could look right into the windows of the second floor--except that the windows were so dirty that he couldn't see much. Suddenly he froze. One of the second-floor windows was being raised. He saw a vague figure behind it, but it was dark in the room and he couldn't see clearly. There was no reason to be disturbed about it, yet he felt a quick wave of apprehension. He had better look over the scratches and get out.

Holding on to the corner girder, he crouched and leaned outward toward the marks. There were two bright scratches about a foot apart. Between them the entire rust surface had been disturbed. Something had rested there, or, more likely, it had been clamped. He swung back a little to look at the inner side of the girder and saw continuations of the scratches that terminated in round spots. When he leaned forward to look at the outer side, the marks were there, but so slight that they wouldn't be noticeable unless one were looking for them.

His brows creased. He couldn't think of anything that would make marks just like those. He wished he had brought a camera. A photo would have given them something to study later.

Then, as he turned and started back, something whistled over his head and slapped sharply into the upright girder. His first thought was that Scotty had thrown a pebble or something to attract his attention, but when he looked, Scotty was facing the other way.

The whistle and slap came again. This time he looked up, and the strength drained from his knees. A few inches over his head were silvery splashes against the rusty surface, and they were the silvery marks of splattered lead!

He was being shot at!

Rick reacted like a suddenly released spring. He dropped to his knees, his hands reaching for a hold on the girder. They hooked over the inner edge and he rolled free on the opposite side. For an instant he dangled in space, then he dropped, his knees flexing to take the shock of landing. It wasn't much of a drop, a little over fourteen feet. And as he dropped he yelled Scotty's name.

Scotty started for him on a dead run, but Rick's yell stopped him.

"Start the boat and cast off!"

Then Rick's legs flew as he ran for the launch. For the moment, both of them were cut off from Creek House by the high board fence. But to get clear they would have to come out of the fence shelter and into the view of the second-floor sniper once more. He planned as he ran, and as he jumped across the water to the launch, he gasped, "Stay close to the reef and pick up speed. Get going."

The launch was already in motion. Rick dropped into the seat next to Scotty and his pal pushed the gas pedal all the way. The nose lifted and the stern dug in.

Rick turned to watch, and as the second floor of Creek House came into view, he said, "Give it all you've got. Cut sharply across Salt Creek and the rushes will cover us."

"Hang on!" Scotty snapped. He threw the wheel hard over and the launch rocked up like a banking plane, then he leveled off and the boat shot across the creek's mouth to safety. Only then did he turn to Rick. "What happened?"

"Someone took two shots at me," Rick replied shakily. "And dollars to dill pickles it was our pal Carrots, because I didn't hear the shots."

"That air rifle," Scotty said. His mouth tightened. "I can't wait to get my hands on that little playmate. Did he miss you by much?"

"About six inches. Both shots hit the same place, within an inch of each other."

Scotty frowned thoughtfully. "Then my guess is that he wasn't trying to hit you. If he's good enough to place two shots like that, he wouldn't have any trouble picking you off. Did you see him?"

"No. I saw a window open just before I got down to look at the marks."

"Anything to them?"

"I don't know," Rick said. He was still a little shaken. "Listen, what about reporting this to the police?"

Scotty shook his head. "No proof. No witnesses. It would be your word against his, because he could claim he was just target practicing and that you weren't on the tower when he fired. He could even claim he didn't fire the shots, because the slugs would be so spattered that the police couldn't make anything of them."

"I can see him laughing his head off," Rick said bitterly. "First, because of dumping the fish scoop, and now because he sent us hightailing out of there like a couple of frightened jack rabbits."

"It would have been stupid to stay and get shot at," Scotty pointed out. "Even if he is a good shot, he might accidentally clip you."

Rick had to admit the truth of that. "Just the same," he said, "we're going back and build a fire under Mister Carrots. Wait and see!"

Chapter 9: Night Watch

Less than a half-hour after arriving at Spindrift, Rick and Scotty were back at Smugglers' Reef. But this time they were in the Cub. With Scotty operating Rick's speed graphic camera, they took several photos of Creek House, Salt Creek, and Brendan's Marsh from varying altitudes. Then Rick swung in a wide circle, losing altitude, and leveled off only a hundred feet over the marsh. He was headed straight for Creek House.

Scotty paused in putting the camera in its case and looked at him.

Rick winked. "I'm going to see if the Kelsos are home."

The Cub flashed across Salt Creek and Rick pulled the control wheel back into his lap. The small plane shot upward in a zoom that just cleared the hotel, then at the top of the zoom Rick did a fast wing over and started back.

"I know you can fly," Scotty said calmly, "but don't try to roll your wheels on the roof."

Rick shot across the hotel within five feet of the chimney and dropped so low that his prop wash flattened the reeds in the marsh. Then, climbing again, he swung wide and went over Seaford at a legal altitude. He was, even the critical Gus admitted, a safe-and-sane flier, but the temptation to get back at Carrots Kelso a little was too much. High over the town, he turned to Scotty. "I didn't see anyone. Now, if you were in the house and a crazy pilot buzzed you twice, what would you do?"

"Run out and look," Scotty said promptly.

"Uhuh." Rick was enjoying himself. Whether his scheme worked or not, he liked it. "And if the plane was out of sight, what would you do then?"

"I'd go far away from the house, so it wouldn't block my view, and look for it."

"The farthest you can get away from Creek House, without running into the fence, is at the end of the pier."

Scotty broke into laughter. "I hope I never have you for an enemy. What'll you bet Carrots doesn't go to the end of the pier?"

"No bets. But I'm hoping."

Rick turned inland. When he was out of sight of the town, he lost altitude in a tight spiral over Salt Creek. At five hundred feet, he banked around and followed the creek, his throttle wide open. As the Cub flashed over Salt Creek Bridge, he put the plane in a shallow dive. Creek House loomed and he let out a yell of triumph.

Carrots Kelso was standing on the end of the pier, looking at the sky!

Rick pointed the nose of the Cub directly at him and held it there. He saw Carrots turn at the noise of the plane, saw his mouth open to yell and his eyes pop. Rick hauled the stick back into his lap and kicked left rudder. As the Cub spun around he banged Scotty with his free hand and chortled with glee.

Carrots, afraid for his life, had gone headlong into the creek.

"That pays him back for shooting at you," Scotty said with satisfaction. "Bet he was more scared than you were. But we still owe him for those fish."

       *   *   *   *   *

Two of the photos proved excellent for their purposes. Scotty, who had taken an interest in developing and printing, made a 10 by 14-inch enlargement of each. They spent most of Thursday studying them, talking over their various clues endlessly, and waiting for Cap'n Mike's call. Shortly after supper on Thursday night he did call, but only to say he had nothing to report and that he hadn't been able to talk to Jim Killian. The fisherman was taking a few days off to visit his mother in Pennsylvania.

"A fine time for him to go vacationing," Rick said, "when he might be able to supply some essential information. I've got an idea, Cap'n," he added. "Can you find out what source the automatic light uses for electricity? See if it has its own power plant or whether there's a cable that runs along the reef. If there is, see if there's a junction box or a switch or anything."

Cap'n Mike promised to have the information next time he called.

They were too restless to sit still and read. Rick had thought about asking his father to help him check the infrared spotlight in the lab, but Hartson Brant was preoccupied with a scientific analysis problem, so Rick decided to check his new invention by actual use.

Dismal was the subject. The boys took him for a walk to the backside of the island where there was no light at all except for dim moonlight. Scotty carried the power supply on a strap over his shoulder while Rick carried the camera and its attachments. The thing was uncanny, even when its operation was understood. To the naked eye, Dismal was just a vague blur under the trees. But with the infrared searchlight on him, Rick could see him through the telescope as though it were white light. He shot a few feet of film, then took it to the photo lab. He could develop short lengths by dipping them into bottles of solution, although full lengths would have to go to a New York lab for processing.

Projecting the test length cleared up his questions. The camera worked beautifully at distances up to three hundred yards. Beyond that, although things still could be seen, the lighting was poor and definition hazy.

He spent more time in the darkroom winding the infrared film on hundred-foot rolls and placing them in light-tight cans, then he reloaded the camera with a full spool. That done, there was nothing to do but wait and try to read.

On Friday night, Scotty glanced up from the leather chair in Rick's room. "What time is it?"

Rick was lying on the bed, studying the ceiling and working on the problem of the tower scratches and the shifting current. He looked at his watch. "Ten of nine. Why?"

"Almost time for the trawlers to be getting back to Seaford."

"As though I didn't know it! Unless we get a call within the next half-hour, we might as well forget it for tonight, too."

Scotty went back to his book. Rick resumed staring at the ceiling. It had occurred to him that there was an old wrecker's trick, well used in the days of sailing ships. The trick was to extinguish a navigation light so ships would run aground and be easy prey for the wreckers. And sometimes the wreckers helped out by raising false lights. Now if the automatic light at the tip of the reef could be cut off, and if a false light were raised on the old tower . . . they just had to talk with Captain Killian! Bill Lake thought a shift of current and a patch of mist had been responsible for him losing the light and putting him off course. But what if Smugglers' Light had been cut off and a false light lighted on the old tower?

Rick snapped his fingers. "I've got it!"

Scotty looked up. "Got what?"

Just then the phone rang.

The boys almost fell over each other in their haste. Rick got to it first and said a breathless hello.

"Cap'n Mike speaking. Rick?"

"Yes!"

"Brad just turned up Salt Creek. I'll be in my shack waiting to hear about it, boy. And say, the automatic light works by a cable. Cable comes down the pole in front of the Creek House fence and goes into a metal box. From there it goes underground to the light."

"Thanks a million," Rick said exultantly. "We'll see you sometime tonight, Cap'n." He hung up and turned to Scotty. "Let's go!"

They ran down the stairs and almost barged into Mrs. Brant. "Got to hurry, Mom."

"Where to, Rick?"

"Seaford," he said. "We'll take the boat. Don't worry, I don't think we'll be out too late."

Mrs. Brant's eyes were troubled. The boys had told the Brants something about events at Seaford. "Be careful, you two," she said.

"We will," Scotty assured her.

They had every intention of being extremely careful. Hartson Brant, who had been on expeditions with the boys, had every confidence in their ability to look out for themselves. But Mrs. Brant, like all mothers, had some reservations.

As they ran down the stairs to the landing, Scotty asked, "What was it you said you had just before the phone rang?"

"Tell you when we get underway," Rick returned, and as they sped through the water at over thirty miles an hour toward Seaford, he did so.

"I think I know how the Sea Belle was wrecked. But if I'm right, the Kelsos were taking a terrific chance."

"They're the kind who take chances." Scotty peered through the windshield at the dark sea. Behind them, their wake was white and turbulent.

"Well, here's how I figure. The Kelsos knew there was no sea traffic off Smugglers' Reef except for the Seaford fleet, because the coastal traffic moves pretty far offshore. They also knew that no one goes down the old road past the hotels at night because there's nothing there. And anyway, if a car came, they could see its lights."

Rick paused. "There's a hole in this theory. In fact, there are a couple of them. I'm guessing that Tom Tyler was the first skipper to get into port a good percentage of the time. If he was, and if they knew it, they could arrange with Brad Marbek to stick close behind him and give them some sort of signal. If they had glasses on the ships, they could see even a flashlight, couldn't they?"

"I suppose so."

"And if they were at the very top of Creek House, in the attic room, they could see the lights of the ships coming in before the ships saw Smugglers'

Light!"

"What are you driving at?" Scotty demanded.

"Smugglers' Light is small. It's strictly for local navigation. Now suppose one of them was in the attic with glasses, waiting for the ships. Tom Tyler comes over the horizon first, Brad Marbek right behind him. Brad makes a signal. Maybe he blinks his masthead light. By that, they know the next ships are pretty far behind and Tom Tyler is in front. The man in the attic signals. They turn off Smugglers' Light from the junction box in front of the hotel and light up their own light on the crossbeam of the old tower. When Captain Tyler comes over the horizon far enough to see the light, what he sees is the Kelsos' light. But he doesn't know that. He gives it leeway as usual; he's used to passing it close because there's plenty of water. Then, when he's within a short distance of it, the light goes off. He keeps on course, thinking something has happened to the light, and piles on the reef."

"And as he piles up, the real light is put back on!" Scotty exclaimed.

"Yes," Rick said excitedly. "And the man with the light in the tower just removes it, gets down, and runs for Creek House before the men on the Sea Belle have even picked themselves up!"

"It makes sense," Scotty agreed. "And how! Of course Tom Tyler knows he's been tricked the minute he hits, and he knows why. So does Brad Marbek, but he's in on it. Bill Lake, who's pretty far behind, thinks the shift in the light is due to a patch of mist and a strong current. But how about Captain Killian? He was closer to the light."

"That's why it's important to get his story," Rick said. His eyes had been scanning the dark coast line ceaselessly. Now, picking up the start of Brendan's Marsh, he turned the wheel and swung out to sea.

Their study of the photographs had convinced them that the best way to approach Creek House was from the rear. To do that, they had to pass far enough out at sea so their engine noise would not be too noticeable and attract the attention of the Kelsos. Rick took a quick look around and saw no other boat lights. He leaned forward and snapped off their own.

In a few moments they saw the lights of Creek House and Smugglers' Light. When they were well past it, Rick turned inshore, throttled down to make as little noise as possible. There was a short dock in front of the abandoned Sandy Shores Hotel. He gauged distance carefully in the dim light and let his momentum carry him to it. Scotty jumped out and made the bow fast while Rick cut the engine completely and hurried to secure the stern. In a moment they were on the dock together looking toward the Creek House.

"Let's go," Rick whispered.

They made their way as noiselessly as possible behind the old hotel, then picked a careful path through accumulated junk past the rears of the Sea Girt, the Atlantic View, and the Shore Mansions. Twice they had to climb rusted fences and Rick was grateful that they had put on old clothes. Presently they were against the Creek House fence.

He touched Scotty's arm and gestured. Then he led the way toward the place where the fence stopped at the marsh. They had planned the adventure up to the end of the fence. After that they would have to take advantage of whatever offered.

They hadn't seen in the photograph that the fence extended into the marsh for a short distance. Rick's first inkling of the fact came when one foot sank into muck above the shoe top. He let out a soft exclamation, and when he pulled the foot free it made a sighing sound.

The boys held a whispered consultation and decided there was nothing for it but to continue. Rick stepped forward, searching with his foot for firmer ground. Now and then he found a hummock, but there were times when he sank to the knee in clinging goo. Fortunately, there were only a few feet of swamp to navigate.

He reached the end of the fence and stopped, peering around it.

There were lights on the pier, and the Albatross was tied up to it, but the lights were too dim to illuminate anything over a few yards away. He crouched and moved over a little, making room for Scotty. Together they surveyed the terrain.

"We can't see much from here," Scotty said, lips against Rick's ear. "We'll have to get closer."

Rick nodded. He motioned along the fence, indicating that they should follow it, then he took the lead again. In a dozen muddy steps they were out of the marshland and on dry ground again, but Rick had to exercise utmost care because there was a litter of dry junk that crackled underfoot. He picked his way carefully, hardly daring to breathe loudly.

Once he froze and felt Scotty tense behind him. Brad Marbek and Red Kelso walked from the hotel to the pier and stood looking upstream. Their backs were to the boys. Rick started moving again. There were no lights in the hotel on the fence side. He wanted to reach the safe darkness of that area before planning their next move. As he went, he wondered where Carrots was, and what had happened to Brad's crew.

They reached the dark space between the hotel and the fence without incident and Rick straightened up with a little breath of relief. Now what? He reviewed the photograph of the hotel grounds in his mind.

Scotty tugged his sleeve and pointed. Rick looked up and saw that a window was open on the first floor. The room behind it was dark. For a second he was tempted, then he shook his head. Going into the hotel was dangerous, even though they probably could make their way to an upper floor and have an unobstructed view from a window. If they were trapped inside ... he didn't like the thought. At least their retreat was open while they were out of doors. The top of the fence was within reach if they jumped. They could swing over it and run. Once outside the fence, the Kelsos would have a hard time catching up with them.

He remembered that the front of the hotel and part of the area on the creek side contained shrubs, relics of its original landscaping. The shrubs would give them cover. He touched Scotty and motioned. Then he started around the front of the hotel, crossing the driveway, which led into the grounds through a gate, closed now and looking like part of the fence.

The front of the hotel was dark. Swiftly he went past the porch, moving through the shrubbery with extreme caution. He gained the corner nearest the creek safely, Scotty behind him. When he peered around, he had a good view of the dock. Red Kelso and Brad Marbek were still talking. No one else was in sight. Somewhere inside, a door banged. Rick stiffened. That must be Carrots, or one of the crew.

He moved forward, spotting a hedge that had marked the edge of the garden. If they crouched behind that, they would have an unobstructed view. He dodged a shrub and reached the hedge; it was just waist-high. He sank to his knees and parted the twigs, searching for a good view through them. Beside him, Scotty knelt and did the same.

He put his mouth close to Scotty's ear. "This is a good place," he whispered.

"It's a fine place," a loud voice said. "Get up, both of you!"

Rick whirled, his heart stopping. He looked straight across the front sight of a rifle into the grinning face of Carrots Kelso!

65

Chapter 10: Captured

"I figured it was time for another look around," Carrots said, "so I came out the side door and went around the back and up the side by the fence, then crossed over by the front. And just as I got to the corner, who did I see, but our two wise-guy pals!" He poked the rifle in Rick's back by way of emphasis.

Red Kelso and Brad Marbek looked at the two boys and then at each other. Marbek looked up the creek nervously. "Better get 'em inside under cover," he said in his high voice. "Jimmy, take 'em into the cabin."

Rick was seething inwardly, but he gave no sign. He was angry with himself. He should have known that there would be a guard.

He walked down the pier, Scotty at his side, the others following. At Carrots' direction he climbed over the side of the trawler and went into the small cabin aft of the wheelhouse.

Red Kelso gestured toward a built-in bunk. "Sit down, both of you." He went to the single window and slid the curtains shut.

Carrots took up a position in the corner from which he could cover the two boys. Brad Marbek pushed into the cabin and closed the door behind him. For a dozen heartbeats there was silence.

Red Kelso broke it. "What now?" he asked heavily. "We've got 'em. What do we do with 'em?"

Rick spoke up with much more boldness than he felt. "Nothing. Half a dozen people know we came here."

Marbek and Kelso exchanged glances.

"We can't just let 'em go," Carrots said. His glance at Rick was vindictive. "This is the smart joker that dove at me in his airplane. I owe him somethin' for that."

"Be quiet, Jimmy," Red Kelso said. "We've got to think about this."

There was a hail from outside. Marbek started. "Red! Come outside. Jimmy, watch these two."

Carrots lifted the rifle a little. The two older men went out and closed the door. Rick, listening carefully, thought he could hear oars.

Scotty spoke up. "You're a good shot with that thing, Rick says. You put two shots right together over his head."

"I should have picked him off," Carrots snarled. "I ought to put a shot in his head right now for makin' me jump off the dock."

"That evened us up," Rick said quietly. "You dumped the fish on us."

Carrots grinned his satisfaction. "You're tootin' I did! And that ain't all I'm goin' to do to you, either."

"Don't be too sure," Scotty said.

Carrots' thin lips tightened. "You got warned. Twice. What happens to you is on your own head."

The door banged open and Red Kelso and Brad Marbek came in again. For some reason they seemed in better spirits. Marbek was grinning.

Kelso stood before the two boys, his seaweed-green eyes surveying them coldly. "All right. Talk. What did you want in here?"

Rick and Scotty remained quiet.

"Don't make me beat it out of you," Kelso warned.

Rick thought quickly. He jerked his thumb at Carrots. "You can blame him. First he dumped half a ton of menhaden on us and then he took a shot at me while I was climbing the old tower."

"Why were you climbin' the tower?" Marbek demanded quickly.

Rick shrugged, nonchalantly, he hoped. "Why does anyone climb a tower? Just for the fun of it."

Carrots snorted. "Nuts! Then why didn't you go all the way to the top?"

Red Kelso's eyes swiveled from his son to the boys. "Let's cut the comedy," he snapped. "Jimmy had nothin' to do with your comin' here. Now give us a straight story or you'll suffer for it!"

Rick's mind was working at top speed. He couldn't tell them everything, but he might be able to stall.

"You warned us," he said. "Twice. Anyway, we thought it was you, then your son just admitted it." He grinned at Kelso. "We had to find out why you were warning us, didn't we?"

Red looked at Carrots and then at Brad. "I told you it was a mistake to try to warn 'em off," he grated. "All right. Did you find out why we warned you?"

"We didn't have time," Scotty pointed out. "We had just arrived when we got caught."

Brad Marbek's high voice was cold. "Do you think my coming here is funny?"

Scotty's reply was equally cold. "You're not trying to kid anyone that you tie up at this pier before unloading your fish just because you want to be sociable,

67

are you?"

Marbek took a step forward. Red Kelso's hand on his shoulder restrained him. Rick held his breath, wondering if Scotty had said too much.

"Okay, you snoopers," Red said. "You're goin' to take a nice long look around, see? You're goin' to do exactly what we say, and you're goin' to find out for yourselves just what's goin' on here. Now how do you like that?"

"Fine," Rick said feebly. There didn't seem to be anything else to say.

"Start at the house," Brad growled. "Get goin'."

On deck, Rick took a quick look around. Nothing had changed, nor was anyone in sight. With Carrots' rifle at their backs, he and Scotty marched to the side door of the hotel. Inside Red Kelso pointed at another door. "Open it and go downstairs. Step on it, we haven't all night."

Rick caught his breath. Why were they forcing them into the cellar? A little fearfully, he went down the stairs as Red snapped on lights.

At the bottom of the steps, the three faced them. "Start lookin'," Brad commanded. "Go on. Stick your noses in every corner. Get busy!" He gave Scotty a shove that sent him staggering in the direction of the coal cellars. Then Red Kelso gave Rick a hard push that landed him on his knees.

The boy stood up again and looked around him uncertainly. "What do you want us to do?"

"Look," Red snapped. "That's what you came for. Look in every blasted corner until you're satisfied there's nothin' more to look for. Now get goin'!"

And Rick and Scotty looked. Even though they knew now nothing would be found in the old house, they had no choice. With the three hovering over them they searched in corners, under stairs, in bins. They sounded walls and rapped floors. As they passed through the kitchen, four men were playing cards, evidently members of Brad's crew. They inspected the butler's pantry and even the refrigerator, then they were pushed on through the other first-floor rooms and up the stairs.

Rick was tired of the whole affair, but every time he hesitated, Brad or Red gave him a headlong shove that kept him moving, and always Carrots was behind with the rifle. When there were no bulbs in the rooms a flashlight Red produced provided illumination. Room by tiresome room they worked their way to the attic.

From the attic they were run down the stairs again and out into the grounds and forced to cover every inch of land. Then they were taken to the garage-

boathouse and made to work their way through what had been the servants'
quarters. Downstairs, they inspected the only car, and Rick automatically made a
mental note of the make and the New York license number. Then they looked
under the seats and into the rope locker of a motor whaleboat that was the only
craft in the boathouse, and they were forced to crawl under the boathouse where
it rested on piles.

"Now," Brad Marbek said grimly, "let's take a look at the trawler."

"Do we have to?" Scotty said wearily. "We know you wouldn't make us look
if there was anything to be seen."

Brad's big hand landed in the middle of his back, smashing him toward the
dock. "March!" he commanded.

The tiresome routine started again. Through wheelhouse and cabin and galley
and enginehouse and rope and gear lockers they hunted, picking up accumulated
layers of dirt and grease on the way, until finally only the huge fish holds were
left.

Rick looked into the forward one and thought, "Oh, no!" He started to protest,
but Brad's open hand caught him on the side of the face. "Dig!" the skipper
commanded. "You asked for it. Dig!"

And dig they did, through tons of stinking menhaden and cold ice until they
choked and their mouths felt full of scales. Once or twice they protested, but
there was always big Brad Marbek ready to strike out and Carrots and Red Kelso
backing him up.

An eternity later they clawed their way up the pile of fish in the last hold.

Rick took a deep breath of clean air. "Anything else?" he asked.

Carrots stepped forward. "You poor jokers got dirty," he said with false
concern. "You need a bath." He pointed to the end of the dock. "Go on, jump in."
His rifle lifted menacingly.

That, at least, was no hardship. Rick walked to the end of the dock and
dropped into the water, savoring is cool cleanliness. Scotty was right beside him.

Overhead, the three waited, and Carrots' rifle was still on them. "Back to the
bank," he commanded.

Rick and Scotty swam, clambered up on shore, and stood waiting.

"Hike."

They were herded like two sheep to the front gate. Red Kelso produced a key
and the gate swung open.

"You had your look," he said. "You came to spy and we helped you out. Now

69

you know there's nothin' wrong here. We warned you because we didn't like you, see? And that's all. Now get goin' and don't ever come back, or we'll work you over so you'll never be the same again. Now git!"

They were shoved violently forward and landed sprawling on the hard macadam road. Behind them the gate slammed shut, and as they got to their feet and looked at each other ruefully, the sound of Carrots' raucous laughter was like salt on raw flesh.

Chapter 11: The Hearing

"You two have certainly got your nerve, going back to Seaford after that," Jerry Webster said.

"We'll stay away from the Kelsos and Brad Marbek. Don't worry about that," Rick assured him. "But we're not giving up, are we, Scotty?"

"Not on your life," Scotty replied flatly.

Jerry's car bounced over Salt Creek Bridge and sped toward the Seaford turnoff. The boys had phoned him early in the morning and found that he had learned about Tom Tyler's hearing during his routine phone calls to the Seaford authorities, and that he was going down to cover it.

They had met him at the Whiteside dock, and on the way down had brought him up to date on their part of the case, including their humiliating experience of the night before.

"So your theory about smuggling must be wrong," Jerry said. "Otherwise, you'd have found something."

"I'm not convinced," Rick argued. "It's still the only answer that fits."

"Then where were the smuggled goods?"

"We could have gotten there too late," Scotty reminded. "If it was a small shipment, it could have been unloaded and disposed of before we showed up."

"Disposed of? How?" Jerry wanted to know.

Rick recalled that he had heard the sound of oars while in the cabin. Red and Brad had rushed out right away, too, after hearing a hail. "They might have taken the stuff up the creek," he mused. "They might even have had a truck waiting at the bridge. There's not much traffic, so it wouldn't be too great a risk. And even if a car came, they could pretend the truck was changing a tire or something until it passed."

"That's reasonable," Jerry admitted. "Did you talk it over with Cap'n Mike?"

Rick grinned ruefully at the memory of the two soaked, bedraggled, filthy specimens who had knocked on Cap'n Mike's door last night. "We were in no mood even to think about it," he said. "But we did find out one thing. Cap'n Mike said it would be easy for anyone to disconnect Smugglers' Light and then reconnect it. All he would need would be an insulated screw driver."

"And that's not all," Scotty added. "He said Tom Tyler was first one back from the fishing grounds eight times out of ten because the Sea Belle was the fastest boat in the fleet and the best handled."

The more Rick thought about it, the more he was convinced that his theory of the wrecking of the trawler would hold water. Cap'n Mike had plugged up another hole, too. Rick had wondered about the backside of the light. He had noticed that there was a red sector on the townside, a common method of construction on lights of that sort. On Cap'n Mike's chart, shaded areas showed how the light worked. It was visible from the seaside in an arc of 180 degrees. It was dark in the quadrant toward the marsh and red in the quadrant toward the town. But warehouses and pier sheds blocked off the light from almost all of the town except Million Dollar Row, and since the red portion would be out for only a short time, it was long odds against anyone noticing it or investigating if they did.

"It's pretty sound," Rick said. "Only I wonder if we'll ever prove it?"

"Not in time for this morning's hearing, that's for sure," Scotty commented. "Maybe Captain Killian will have something to say. If he ever gets back."

Cap'n Mike had tried unsuccessfully last night to see Jim Killian. He was still visiting his mother.

Jerry's car rolled down the main street of Seaford toward the town hall. Rick could see that an unusual number of cars was lined up along the curbs. The hearing was attracting a great deal of interest, as could have been expected. He wondered if the Kelsos would be there.

Jerry pulled into a convenient parking space. As they got out, he asked Rick, "Got your camera?"

Rick held it up. "We've got our press cards, too. That makes us legal spectators for a change."

"For a change is right," Scotty said. "Lead the way, Jerry."

The hearing room was on the second floor. Jerry pushed his way through the crowd in the corridor with Rick and Scotty following, and found the entrance. A police officer stopped them at the door, then permitted them to enter when they showed their press cards. Rick wondered if the hearing would be closed to the public, but when he got inside he saw that every seat was taken. He recognized a face here and there, including that of Bill Lake. The others he recognized were fishermen he had seen during their trip to the pier with Cap'n Mike. Evidently some of them were taking the day off because of the hearing.

The room was actually a small courtroom. Like most courtrooms, it had a low fence dividing the spectators from the participants. At a table inside the fence, Tom Tyler was seated with four other men. Rick guessed from their appearance that they must be the members of his crew. One had an arm in a sling and he remembered Cap'n Mike had said the wreck had caused one broken arm.

Jerry spoke to a man who seemed to be someone of authority, and they were directed to seats in the front row. Across the aisle Rick saw Mrs. Tyler and the little girl who had been with her on that first night. The captain's wife looked pale, but she seemed composed. Then he switched his glance to the captain himself.

Tom Tyler seemed thinner in the few days since the wreck of his ship. He stared at the table before him, seemingly oblivious to the murmur of voices in the room. Rick felt compassion for him. If the theory proved correct, Tom Tyler was the victim of unscrupulous men who had wrecked his ship deliberately, just to remove danger from their path.

He speculated about what might have caused the actual decision to wreck the Sea Belle . There was only one sensible conclusion. Captain Tyler must have used the trawler to spy on Brad Marbek. Wrecking the ship would serve a double purpose: it would remove the possibility of further spying on Brad and it would warn Tyler that the smugglers meant business. After that, simply telling him that his family would suffer if he kept on would strike home. Until the wreck, he probably had been inclined to treat Kelso's warning lightly.

A door to the left of the judge's rostrum opened and three men came out. One was a Coast Guard commander. The other two were civilians. A whisper from Jerry informed Rick that they were officers of the United States Maritime Commission.

Rick turned to see if the Kelsos or Brad Marbek were in the room. He was curious about Cap'n Mike, too. While he was searching the rows of faces, the procedure started. A clerk got up and announced something about the hearing being held before the duly authorized board of inquiry in the case of the wrecking on Smugglers' Reef of the motor vessel Sea Belle , of so many tons, and such and such a registry number, Thomas Lee Tyler, master, holding licenses numbers so and so. Jerry nudged Rick and pointed to the camera. Rick nodded and inserted a flash bulb. He caught the clerk's eye and held up the camera. The clerk frowned, then motioned him to come inside the rail. Rick did so and snapped a picture of the tribunal. Then he turned and got a photo of Tom Tyler and the men at his table, with the audience in the background. He looked at Jerry. The young reporter nodded, indicating that two pictures would be enough.

Rick resumed his seat.

The middle man on the platform leaned over and asked, "Who is representing Captain Tyler?"

Tom Tyler stood up. "No one sir."

A murmur ran through the courtroom.

"Captain," the man asked, "do you mean you have come into this hearing without counsel?"

"Sir, I'm pleading guilty to whatever the charge is. I don't need a lawyer for that." Tyler sat down again.

There was whispered consultation among the three on the bench. Then the spokesman leaned forward again.

"Captain, as I understand the facts presented by the officers who investigated, if you plead guilty you will, in effect, state that you deliberately wrecked your ship. If you so state, your insurance company will have no recourse but to ask your arrest on a charge of barratry. Do you understand that?"

Tyler's shoulders straightened. "If that's the way it is, sir, I guess that's the way it is. I'm pleading guilty."

The murmur in the court rose.

Rick leaned over to Jerry. "He's scared stiff. He must be, to take this lying down."

But if the Kelsos had threatened Mrs. Tyler and their little girl, there wasn't much else he could do. Wrecking the trawler had shown him they were capable of carrying out any threat. Rick was glad he had had presence of mind the night before to say that other people knew he and Scotty were going to Creek House. He was sure that had the Kelsos and Brad thought that no one else knew, their fate would have been much different.

A hand fell on his shoulder. He looked up into the face of the officer who had been at the door.

"You Rick Brant?"

He nodded.

"Cap'n Mike is outside. Says it's urgent. He wants you and Don Scott."

"We'll come right away," Rick said. He leaned over and explained to Jerry. "We'll meet you outside. Come on, Scotty."

As quietly as possible he and Scotty left the room just as the spokesman for the board declared that the hearing would proceed.

Cap'n Mike was on the steps in front of the town hall. His weathered face lit up at the sight of the boys and he greeted them with a note of worry in his voice. "Come on down to the sidewalk out of earshot of these folks," he said in a low tone.

They followed him to a place where the crowd thinned out, then Rick asked, "What's the matter, Cap'n? Anything important come up?"

"Important? I'll say it's important!" Cap'n Mike leaned forward. "Jim Killian has disappeared!"

Chapter 12: The Missing Fisherman

Captain Jim Killian, the fisherman who had been closest to Brad Marbek and Tom Tyler, and who might have been able to say finally whether Rick's theory was true or not, was missing!

"Cap'n, are you sure?" Rick asked.

Cap'n Mike nodded soberly. "Sure as I can be. That's why I had to talk to you boys."

"When did you discover he had disappeared?" Scotty queried. "You said he had been visiting his mother."

"That's just it. Took me all this time to remember." Cap'n Mike shook his white head. "Reckon I'm getting old. His mate said he'd gone to visit his mother, so I thought no more about it. Until this morning. Then I remembered. Jim Killian never knew his mother. He was brought up by an uncle and aunt, both of them dead ten years now. Struck me all of a sudden. It had sort of been nagging at the back of my head that something was fishy about that mate's story anyway, so this morning I went to his house and I collared him."

"Did you get anything out of him?" Rick asked eagerly.

"Not much. Jim Killian showed up at his trawler the morning after Tom Tyler wrecked the Sea Belle. He just told the mate to shove off without him, and said if anyone asked, he was visiting his mother, who was sick. And I'm sure that's all the mate knows, except that he knew Jim Killian didn't have a mother."

Rick pursed his lips thoughtfully. "He showed up himself? Then he must have left of his own free will. At least he wasn't kidnapped. But why would he run away?"

His eyes met Scotty's and he knew his pal was thinking the same thing.

"He was threatened," Scotty said.

"Looks like it. Suppose he had let a word drop that night about something being a little off the beam about Smugglers' Light?" It sounded reasonable to Rick. "The Kelsos would have paid him a visit for sure."

Cap'n Mike wagged his head sadly. "I sure pinned a lot of hope on Jim Killian. After you explained what might have happened to Tom, I was sure Jim might have something real useful to add. But it looks mighty bad now."

76

"Mighty bad," Rick agreed. Their effort to catch the Kelsos red-handed had boomeranged on them and now what might be proof of their theory had vanished.

"We'd better find him," Scotty said.

"How?" Cap'n Mike asked hopelessly. "We can't go to the police, 'cause Jim went off of his own will, which he has a perfect right to do."

For a moment Rick was about to suggest that they could have the police hunt him as a material witness, then he rejected the idea. Witness to what? Tom Tyler had admitted running the Sea Belle on the reef purposely, or next thing to it. No, the only solution was to find Captain Killian. But where to begin?

"Put yourself in his place," he suggested to Cap'n Mike. "You've known him a long time. If you were hiding out, where would you go?"

"I've thought about it," the old seaman said. "Don't do no good. This is the first time Jim Killian has left town in twenty years, except to go into Newark or New York for a day's shopping."

"Where did he live?" Scotty asked.

"Little Cape Cod cottage over near Tom Tyler. Lived by himself."

"We might start there," Rick said.

"Good a place as any," Cap'n Mike agreed. "Let's get going."

Rick shook his head. "We have to wait for Jerry. Let's sit in the car. I don't think the hearing will last very long. Tom Tyler is pleading guilty."

They walked to Jerry's car and settled down to wait. Through the windshield Rick watched the townfolk clustered around the courthouse steps and noted that they weren't talking much. He guessed everyone in town knew there was something extraordinary about the wreck of the Sea Belle and he wondered if anyone suspected smuggling activities at Creek House.

He said aloud, "If the Kelsos and Brad Marbek took the stuff up to Salt Creek Bridge before we got there, what boat did they use? The boat we saw in the boathouse was dry, and the boats on the Albatross were hanging on the davits. Maybe we're all wet on that, too."

"Maybe," Scotty agreed glumly. "I've never seen a deal with so many dead ends."

Cap'n Mike sounded alarmed. "You're not giving up, are you, boys?"

"Not a chance. We'll get to the bottom of this sooner or later." Scotty spoke for both of them.

Cap'n Mike pointed. "The crowd's coming out."

Evidently the hearing was over, because those who had waited inside the building and those lucky enough to get seats were coming out. Presently Jerry Webster came out, too, tucking his notes into his jacket pocket. He joined them in the car and greeted Cap'n Mike.

"You look like three mourners," he told them. "What's the matter?"

Rick explained briefly, then asked, "Got any bright ideas?"

"Afraid not," Jerry replied. "Finding someone is a tough job even for the police with all their facilities. I don't know how you'd even start."

"We thought of looking his house over," Rick said.

"I wouldn't do that," Jerry replied quickly.

"Why not?"

"You said he left of his own accord, didn't you? You can bet he locked his house up tight. If you try to get in, you'll be guilty of breaking and entering. And even if he left a door open, you've no right to go in. You can bet the neighbors will be on the phone to the constable's office if they see anyone fooling around the house."

"You're right," Rick agreed gloomily.

"There goes his mate now," Cap'n Mike said. "Must have been at the hearing." He pointed to a slender man in a cap and lumberjack's shirt who was crossing the street in front of town hall.

"Think he told you all he knows?" Rick asked.

Cap'n Mike rubbed his chin thoughtfully. "Don't know. Maybe he did, and again maybe not. Chick's a quiet one. Never says much and there's no way of telling what goes on inside his head."

"Let's follow him," Scotty suggested.

Jerry looked at him. "What for?"

"For lack of anything else to do," Scotty said. "Can't tell. We've nothing to lose, anyway."

Rick watched the mate reach the opposite sidewalk, then stand uncertainly for a moment, looking back across the street. Then, evidently satisfied, he started off at a brisk walk. It was almost as though he had looked to see if anyone were coming after him, Rick thought.

"Scotty's right," he said quickly. "Let's go after him."

Jerry started the car and pulled away from the curb. He grinned at Rick. "Good thing it's Saturday. No paper until Monday morning, so I've plenty of time. But tell me what to do. I'm green at this business."

"Go slow," Rick said. "Watch him."

78

The mate reached a corner, looked behind him, then turned down the side street.

"Go after him," Rick directed. "Go right on by him and don't anyone look at him. Cap'n, better crouch down. He knows you, but he doesn't know the rest of us."

Jerry swung into the side street and picked up speed. From the corner of his eye Rick saw the mate walking rapidly. He told Jerry to turn right at the next corner and to slow down. The blocks were short; the mate would pass the corner in a moment.

"Do you know where he lives?" Rick asked the captain.

"Not on this side of town. He lives out in the district toward the main road."

"Any guesses about where he might be heading?"

"Maybe Jake's Grill. It's this way and I've seen him there."

Rick directed Jerry to go on to the next corner and wait. Then he turned and watched the corner they had just passed. If the mate kept straight on the side street, they would go around the block. If he turned down the street they had taken, they would simply round the corner again.

The mate turned and came after them.

"Around the corner," Rick directed. "Cap'n, where is this Jake's Grill?"

"If you'd turned left instead of right just then," Cap'n Mike replied as Jerry finished the turn, "you'd have been about at it. It's halfway down the block."

Rick made a quick decision. "Okay, here's where we split up. I'll get out and go to Jake's. The rest of you keep trailing him. If he goes into Jake's, turn around and park at the next corner where you can see the entrance. If he doesn't, follow him and pick me up later."

As they nodded assent, he got out of the car and waved Jerry on, then he walked swiftly in the opposite direction. He crossed the street from which they had just turned, and caught a glimpse of the mate from the corner of his eye. The man was still walking rapidly. Rick paid no attention to him. He walked at a moderate pace down the street, pausing once to look in a shop-window. A side glance showed him the mate, still coming. Rick resumed walking and came to Jake's Grill, a shabby sort of place with only a half dozen customers. He walked in without hesitation and took a seat at the counter.

The counterman came up and wiped the counter clean in front of him with a rag that might have been white once upon a time. "What'll it be?"

"Coffee," Rick said. He was in a good position, because the back of the counter was lined with a flyspecked mirror through which he could see the whole restaurant.

The mate pushed the door open and paused at the entrance. He reached in his pocket and brought out a crumpled handful of bills and some change. He counted the change, then searched the pocket for more. There was none. He started for the counter.

He must need more change. For what? Rick's quick survey of the place showed him a phone booth in one corner. Quickly, as the mate approached, he fished out a dollar and thrust it at the counterman. "Got any change? I have to make a phone call."

The counterman took the bill and walked to the cash register. The mate cast a quick glance at Rick, then called, "Sam, I need some change, too. Give me some nickles and dimes for this half-buck." He tossed a fifty-cent piece on the counter.

Rick relaxed. Perhaps some of the townfolk had seen his and Scotty's pictures in the paper, but evidently the mate wasn't one of them. There had been no recognition in the man's eyes.

The counterman handed Rick a dollar in change and gave the mate some smaller change. He winked. "Gotta call yer girl, Chick?"

"Sure have," the mate answered. He had an odd voice, as though his nasal passages were completely blocked with a bad cold. He looked at Rick. "Go ahead, kid, make your call."

"After you, sir," Rick said politely. "I'm in no hurry."

"Thanks." The mate walked to the booth and shut himself in.

Rick got up and wandered casually in that direction, his ears cocked for the mate's words. Unfortunately, the booth was tight. He could hear only a faint murmur. He went back to the counter and started sipping his coffee, keeping his eyes on the booth. He heard the dim tone of bells and his pulse quickened. Those were coins dropping into the slots. The mate was making an out-of-town call! If only he could hear!

The hot coffee was almost scalding, but he scarcely noticed. His mind was racing, searching for some way to overhear that conversation. There just wasn't any way. If he walked over and put his ear to the booth, the men sitting at the tables and farther up the counter would see. No, he was sunk this time.

Within four minutes the mate was out of the booth. He came over and took a seat at the counter a few stools up and nodded at Rick. "Thanks, boy."

"That's all right," Rick said. He had to make a pretense of phoning now. Well, he could call Spindrift and tell his mother they would be home for lunch. He hadn't been sure how long the hearing would take when they left.

He went into the booth and closed the door. The phone had no dial. Evidently Seaford, like Whiteside, had no dial system. He started to pick up the receiver and inspiration struck him. If he could imitate the mate...

He tried to imitate Chick's nasal tone and thought he did pretty well. He tried again, and it sounded a little better. Anyway, he thought, there was nothing to lose by trying. If Seaford had more than one operator on the town switchboard, which was unlikely because of the size of the town, it wouldn't work, anyway. Or, if there were two and he got the wrong one it wouldn't work.

His hand shook slightly as he lifted the receiver and dropped in his nickel.

"Number, please?" the operator said sweetly.

Rick struggled to imitate the mate's voice. "Say, I have to talk to that number again. Something I forgot to say."

"What number was that, sir?" the operator asked.

Rick took a chance, based on the number of bells he had heard.

"That New York number," he said. "Forget now what it is. Ain't you got it written down there?"

"I'll have to have the number, sir," the operator said with firm sweetness.

Rick grew desperate. "Shucks, lady," he whined nasally. "You ain't goin' t'make me go through that business with that information gal again, are you?"

There was a subdued tinkle of laughter. "All right. I'll find it." There was a brief pause. "That number is Cornish 9-3834. Better write it down this time."

"I sure will," Rick said. He almost forgot and lapsed back into his own voice. But he didn't have to write it down. He wasn't forgetting it.

"What is your number, please?"

He gave it, then waited anxiously. In a moment a voice said, "Garden View Hotel."

The operator spoke. "One moment, please. Please deposit thirty cents."

Rick did so, and the bells clanged in his ear. When the ringing stopped, he said briskly, "Mr. James Killian, please."

"Just a minute." Then, "No one registered here by that name."

"Isn't this the Garden Arms Apartments?" Rick asked.

"No. This is the Garden View Hotel. You have the wrong number."

"Oops, sorry," Rick said jubilantly, and hung up.

He walked to the counter and gulped his coffee, put a dime on the counter and then hurried to the door. The mate was eating a piece of pie.

On the street, Rick looked for Jerry's car and spotted it at a corner two blocks away. He walked rapidly toward it, waving as he did so. The car pulled away from the curb and sped toward him, and he motioned to Jerry to turn the next corner. He hurried and got there just as the car did.

"Any luck?" Scotty asked.

"Luck? Touch me, somebody. Listen to this: Captain Killian is at the Garden View Hotel in New York, registered under a phony name!" He told them quickly what had happened in the grill and finished, "I'll bet the mate had orders to phone right after the hearing and let Killian know what had happened to Tyler."

"He was handed over to the constable after the insurance company issued a complaint," Jerry said. "Forgot to tell you that. Well, we know where this missing captain is. Now what?"

"Now what! What do you think?" Rick asked indignantly. "Let's go to New York!"

Chapter 13: The Tracker

"We can drop your pictures off at the office, then I'll drive you in to New York, if that's okay," Jerry remarked, as the car sped up the road to Whiteside.

"That will be fine," Rick said. "I'll phone Spindrift, too, and let Mom know we won't be home for lunch. We can pick up a hamburger at a roadstand on the way in."

Jerry slowed down to a more moderate pace and Rick looked at him, surprised. "Thought we were in a hurry."

"Trying something," Jerry said. His eyes were on the rearview mirror. After a moment he spoke. "The car behind us slowed down, too. I think he's following us."

Cap'n Mike started to look back, but Scotty said warningly, "Don't! If they're really following, we don't want to let them know they've been spotted."

"There's a curve up ahead, Jerry," Rick said. "Keep your eyes on that car as we round the curve and let me know when they're out of sight."

"Okay."

The curve loomed. Jerry took it smoothly, then glanced up at the mirror. "Now," he said.

Rick reached up and readjusted the mirror so he could see, then settled back. In a few seconds the other car was in sight, too far back for him to see the figures on the license plate, but not so far that he couldn't see clearly that the plate was from New York, or that the car was the same make and model as the one they had seen in Kelso's garage. Reflection of light on the windshield made the occupant hazy, but Rick had a good idea who it was.

"Looks like Kelso's car," he told the others. "Listen, Jerry, don't go to the paper. Drop us in front of Dean's Department Store, then go around the block. Go slowly to give us time to find out who this bird is. No, I've got a better idea. Park the car. He'll have to park his if he intends to follow us."

Jerry nodded agreement. "There's a parking lot next to the store. I'll swing in there."

Cap'n Mike was grinning from ear to ear. "I'll be dadblamed if this ain't just like something I read once," he said. "I knew if I got you two interested we'd have some excitement!"

Jerry chuckled. "What do you think I want to take them into New York for? I usually go swimming on Saturday afternoon."

They were at the outskirts of Whiteside now. Jerry slowed speed again, and three minutes later he swung into the parking lot next to Dean's, in the busiest part of the town. Through the rearview mirror Rick saw the other car go by, heading for a vacant space at the curb, probably. He had noticed one a half block down.

The four got out of the car and Jerry took the parking check from the attendant. "Now what?" he asked.

"We walk down the street," Rick directed, "and if we haven't spotted him by the time we get to Mark's Supermarket, turn into the store. It has two entrances."

"If we split up, he'd get confused and we'd lose him easy," Jerry suggested. "Then we could meet somewhere."

"Amateur," Scotty scoffed. "We don't want to lose him. We want to find out who he is."

Rick and Scotty led the way, Cap'n Mike and Jerry following. As they passed the parked car, Rick saw the license plate clearly. It was the one he had noticed at Kelso's. Probably Carrots or Red, he thought. Maybe both. Without seeming to look around, he noted every possible hiding place where the tracker might wait for them, and decided on the doorway of an office building. There were a half dozen pillars the tracker could use for cover. He waited until they were a half block down from the building, then he turned suddenly as though to speak to the two behind him. Scotty, whose mind worked much the same way, turned at about the same time.

Rick got a quick glimpse of a stocky youth with carrot hair dodging into a doorway. He stopped and said, "Don't look back. I've got him spotted. Let's go into Mark's and we'll figure out how to get rid of him."

"Carrots," Scotty said gleefully. "We'll have to think of something really cute for that little friend."

"Fiend," Rick corrected.

They turned into the supermarket and mingled with the shoppers. Rick led the way behind a counter stacked high with cereals where they couldn't be seen. "The meeting is open to suggestions," he said. "We can shake him with no trouble, but that's too good for him. Any ideas?"

"Lead him on a wild-goose chase," Jerry offered.

Scotty had a grin on his face that boded ill for Carrots Kelso. "I've got one. I saw it pulled once. Jerry, do you suppose Mildred is at the office?"

Mildred Clark, the older sister of one of Barby Brant's closest friends, was the newspaper's bookkeeper. She had been a visitor at Spindrift several times, accompanying Jerry to picnics or swimming parties.

Jerry looked at his watch. "It's Saturday afternoon, and she usually doesn't work, but we're getting out our monthly statements, so she's probably there."

"Swell. Now how well do you know the cop on this beat?"

"We're good friends. I gave him a plug in the paper once. He deserved it, but he thinks I did it out of the goodness of my heart."

Scotty's grin widened. He lowered his voice and rapidly sketched the part each was to play. As he talked, Rick, too, began to grin.

When Scotty had finished, Rick and Cap'n Mike sauntered to the front of the store. Rick glanced through the big plate-glass windows, but he saw no sign of Carrots. That meant nothing, because Carrots would be a complete cabbagehead to let himself be seen. Rick was sure he was watching. He and Cap'n Mike stood talking for a moment, then Scotty appeared beside them, and said, "Well, here goes--Jerry's on the phone now," and faded into the crowd again.

Rick let five minutes elapse while he and the Captain stood in plain sight, then he glanced at his watch and motioned to the old seaman. The two of them went out the front of the store. Long before this, Scotty and Jerry had gone through the side entrance that opened on another street.

Rick waited in front of the store, glancing in now and then, and trying to act impatient. Then he and the Captain started up Main Street at a slow walk. If everything was working out, Carrots would have chosen to follow them rather than to wait at the store for Scotty and Jerry. That was what Rick would have done in his place. He had a hunch Carrots had picked them up in Seaford and had followed them largely because of Cap'n Mike's presence. It was entirely possible that the Kelsos were equally anxious to know of Captain Killian's whereabouts. Or perhaps they were just interested in seeing if Cap'n Mike knew where he was.

As they passed Dean's Department Store, Rick glanced into the doorway and saw Mildred Clark. He breathed a little easier. The others had made it on time. And coming down the street toward him was the policeman who always patrolled this beat. Although he knew Rick well, he made no sign.

They neared the entrance of the parking lot and Jerry motioned from behind a car. He was peering down the street behind them. "Watch this!" he said gleefully, and stepped into plain view.

Rick whirled just as Carrots Kelso came abreast of Dean's doorway. Mildred stepped out ahead of him. She was a slender, attractive girl, and a good actress, as it proved. She was pulling on gloves, and as is usually the case while so doing, she had her purse tucked under her arm.

She and Carrots were only a yard apart when Scotty appeared from the doorway. He took a long step past Carrots, snatched Mildred's purse from under her arm, whirled, and handed it to the astonished redhead. Carrots' reaction was perfect. He took the purse stupidly and stood there with his mouth open.

Scotty vanished back into the doorway. Mildred screamed.

Carrots saw immediately that he was being framed. He turned to run, but forgot to let go of the purse. Mildred screamed again and Carrots sprinted headlong into Duke Barrows. Duke held him for the moment it took for the policeman to arrive.

It was too good to miss. Rick, Jerry, and the Captain walked back down the street toward the confusion, trying hard to conceal their mirth.

Mildred pointed at the purse Carrots still clutched. "That," she proclaimed dramatically, "is my purse!"

"I didn't take it," Carrots yelled. "Someone handed it to me!"

The officer scowled. "A likely story! Unless you had a confederate. Where is he?"

Quite a crowd was gathering now. Mildred turned convincingly faint and Duke had to prop her up. Rick's face was scarlet from choking back laughter, because he was sure Carrots would burst from sheer anger at any moment.

Then Carrots saw him. "You!" he screamed and jerked the policeman's arm. "There he is! That's one of them. His friend took my--I mean it was his friend who--"

The officer interrupted. "Do you know this boy?" he asked Rick.

Rick shook his head, his face solemn. "Never saw him before in my life," he said calmly.

Jerry spoke in a stage whisper that could have been heard a block. "A perfect criminal type if I ever saw one."

Cap'n Mike choked and had to turn away.

Rick nudged Jerry and they turned and walked rapidly back to the parking lot. It was time to get going.

Scotty was standing by the car, grinning broadly. Cap'n Mike was weak from laughing. "Y'know," he chortled, "I've heard the word 'ham' used for actors, but I never got the full meaning until now. Never saw such bad acting in my life, except for the girl. She was almost convincing."

"On our way," Rick said, and laughter bubbled up as they got into the car. As they pulled out into the traffic, they saw Carrots being marched up the street toward the police station, Duke and Mildred walking behind him and the policeman.

"Duke phoned the chief from the paper," Jerry said. "They'll go through all the motions of booking Carrots and taking his picture, then they'll throw him in a cell for a while. When he quiets down, the chief will go in and talk to him like a father and point out that crime doesn't pay, then he'll let him go with a warning."

Scotty sobered. "It worked like a charm," he said. "But Rick, old egg, from now on you and I had better stay away from the front end of Carrots' little air gun!"

Chapter 14: Captain Killian

Jerry turned down the cross street and looked around him doubtfully. "I don't know what a fancy hotel would be doing in this neighborhood, Rick."

"We don't know how fancy it is," Rick returned. "It just has a fancy name. But keep going. We should get to it soon. See any numbers?"

They had stopped and found the address in a telephone book as soon as they crossed the river into New York through the Holland Tunnel. As Jerry pointed out, it wasn't a likely neighborhood in which to find a hotel. It seemed to be mostly manufacturing plants engaged in making gloves and ladies clothes.

"Wonder how he happened to choose this location?" Scotty asked.

"Probably just came into the city and walked down this way and went into the first hotel he saw," Cap'n Mike speculated. "Man gets used to a fishing trawler, he's not going to ask for anything fancy by way of a hotel."

Jerry and Rick had been scanning the numbers along the street. "It's on your side," Rick said. "Watch for it."

Jerry applied the brakes and the car slowed. "That must be it," he said, pointing across the street.

It wasn't what Rick had expected. A tiny metal sign announced that this was the Garden View Hotel. It was set above a dingy doorway through which a flight of stairs could be seen.

"Where's the garden it's supposed to have a view of?" Scotty wanted to know.

Rick motioned in the general direction of uptown. "Probably Madison Square Garden. You could see it from here easily if there weren't about two thousand buildings in the way including the Empire State." He was wondering if they had the right place. "This calls for a small change in plans," he said.

On the way to New York they had decided it would be easiest to give a bellhop a generous tip and have him locate Captain Killian for them. Bellhops usually knew about every guest in a small hotel, and they suspected the Garden View would be small simply because none of them had ever heard of it.

"You're right," Scotty agreed. "A place like that wouldn't have a bellhop."

Rick searched for an idea. "You wouldn't know his signature on the register, would you. Cap'n?"

"Never seen him sign his name."

"Why couldn't one of us be a relative looking for him?" Jerry offered.

"Say, that's an idea!" Scotty exclaimed. "We could pretend he's a little cracked and describe him. The clerk would know who we meant, and he'd probably be glad to tell us, because hotels don't like having people who might be a little bit off."

"Cap'n Mike could do it," Rick said. "Cap'n, couldn't you pretend to be his brother?"

"Sure I could. Well, what are we waiting for? Do I go alone?"

"I'll go with you," Rick offered.

"Jerry and I had better wait, then," Scotty said. "It might look funny if four of us came trooping in like a chowder-and-marching club."

Jerry spoke up. "That's okay, except don't forget I'm to talk with him if he has anything to say. Have to get an interview for the paper."

"We'll bring him down," Rick promised confidently. "Let's go, Cap'n."

The stairs leading up into the hotel were creaky with age, and the accumulation of dust and dirt showed months without a broom. At the top of the stairs was what had once been quite a nice lobby. But now the rug was worn to strings and the wallpaper had acquired a glaze of dirt that made it look like ancient newspapers. Behind the scarred ruin of an oak counter stood a clerk so fat Rick wondered how the floor could support him. He was reading a comic book, and he didn't even look up as they came in.

Cap'n Mike addressed him politely. "Excuse me, sir. I wonder if you can help me."

Tired eyes looked up from the comic book. "What can I do for you?" The words and tone were surprisingly courteous.

"I'm looking for my brother," Cap'n Mike said. "He's a man about my height, five years younger, still a lot of black in his hair. Red complexion, pretty well lined, smokes a corncob pipe. His real name is Killian, but I don't think you'd know him by that." He touched his head significantly. "Mind is going. He thinks he's being persecuted."

"What makes you think he might be here?"

Cap'n Mike's expressive face assumed a look of infinite sadness. "Once, many years ago, he spent his honeymoon here. Lost his wife shortly after in an auto crash, but since his mind went he won't believe she's dead. Even though it was nigh onto twenty years ago. Poor soul. Keeps looking for her. We try to keep him

89

home, so he sneaks off and takes an assumed name. Found him here once before."

"When?" the tone was suspicious. "I've been here five years myself, and I don't remember anything like that."

"Oh, it was longer ago than that," Cap'n Mike added hastily. "Must be over eight." He coughed apologetically. "We've had him in an old seaman's home for a few years, but he wasn't happy there."

Rick looked at Cap'n Mike with admiration. When it came to spinning a convincing yarn right off the cuff, so to speak, Cap'n Mike was a master. Rick hid a smile. What had the old man said about ham actors a little while back?

The clerk was nodding slowly. "Old seaman, is he? Well, that fits one of our guests." He looked at Cap'n Mike sharply. "Sure it's all right? Who is this boy?"

Cap'n Mike put his hand on Rick's shoulder. "This? Ah, sir, it's this boy's poor mother old Jim came here to find."

Rick bowed his head and looked as sad as possible. He had to bow it anyway, to conceal the grin that was forcing its way to the surface.

"What room is he in?" Cap'n Mike asked tenderly. "Poor old soul."

"I'll call him." The clerk went to the switchboard and plugged in a line, then pulled the toggle switch a couple of times. He picked up the phones and put them on. "Mr. Jameson? Your brother and son are down here to see you."

Rick held his breath.

The clerk unplugged the line and put the phone down. "He'll be downstairs in a minute." He went back to his comic book.

Rick and Cap'n Mike went over to a sofa and sat down. As they did so, a little cloud of dust rose.

The minutes ticked away. Rick fidgeted.

He leaned over close to Cap'n Mike. "What do you suppose is keeping him?"

"Don't know," Cap'n Mike whispered back. "We'd better see." He rose and walked to the desk again. "He's slow in coming, sir. I'm just wondering. Remember I said he thought we were persecuting him? He may ... well, sir, I wonder if we could go up?"

There was a trace of alarm in the clerk's face. "Maybe you better," he agreed. "Room 410. Three flights. Two floors up."

Rick and the Captain hurried for the stairs, went up them two at a time. To Rick's surprise the old man kept pace with him. On the fourth landing they paused and looked up and down the shabby corridor. One door was open. Rick ran to it and looked at the number. It was 410. He rushed into the room, a tiny box with only a bed, a washstand and a closet. It was empty. He flung the closet door open and saw a suitcase.

"He's gone," he called, and rushed back into the hall again. Cap'n Mike already was trying other doors. All of them were locked except the bath, and that was empty.

Rick ran the other way, to the end of the hall where a window stood open. Fire escape! He leaned far out the window and looked down into a maze of back alleys. Then his searching eyes saw a figure scurrying through them, heading east.

"Cap'n," he called. "Hurry downstairs! Tell Jerry to cut around the block. He's heading east, the same way the car is. I'll go after him!" He swung a leg through the window and jumped to the steel fire escape as Cap'n Mike rushed for the stairs.

Rick went down the open steel stairs as though he had wings. As he passed the second floor, he saw the clerk's mouth open to call. Rick didn't wait to see what he had to say. Perhaps he was trying to tell him Captain Killian had gone down, too. The clerk would have seen him. Rick shook his head. The captain must have waited on the fire escape until they started up the stairs in order to avoid being seen through the window.

The last flight was counterbalanced. He stepped on the stairs and they swung down with a faint groan. Then he was on the ground. He turned east and ran, leaping over fallen trash and barrels. He had a picture of the alleys in his mind, so he took all the right turns but one. That one brought him into a dead end. He backtracked quickly and found the right way out, and in a moment he came out on the avenue. He stopped on the curb and looked both ways, spying Jerry's car on the uptown side, cruising along slowly. He started to call, then realized Jerry wouldn't hear him. Better to wait. If the car hadn't reached the avenue before Captain Killian, it was a good bet that they had lost him. He scuffed his shoe on the curb disgustedly.

Jerry swung into the next cross street, apparently with the intention of going completely around the block. And Rick saw a figure step out of a doorway the moment the coast was clear! The man fitted the description Cap'n Mike had given. Rick turned his back hurriedly and walked leisurely in the opposite direction. Then he turned into an alley between two buildings and peered out. Captain Killian was walking briskly uptown. Rick saw him turn right at the next corner, in the direction opposite from that Jerry had taken.

Once Killian was out of sight, Rick turned and ran uptown, crossing the avenue. At the corner the seaman had turned, he slowed and looked around cautiously. It was a long block. The captain was about halfway down it. Rick debated. Jerry, if he had gone around the block, would appear on the avenue in a moment, probably one block farther up, since he wouldn't retrace the street in front of the hotel.

Rick decided to take the chance. This part of town was almost deserted, because it was late in the afternoon, and few offices were open on Saturdays, anyway. They could spot Killian easily enough now that he knew which direction he had taken. He ran to the next corner and had to wait only a few seconds before Jerry's car appeared across the street. He put fingers to his mouth and gave a piercing whistle. Jerry tooted the horn and shot across the avenue to him as the light turned green.

"Straight ahead," Rick said. "With luck, we'll meet him at the corner, unless he turned downtown."

The car roared through the narrow street to the next corner and stopped. Rick and Cap'n Mike piled out, and the Captain went to meet the man who had stopped short at their sudden appearance.

"Howdy, Jim," he said.

Captain Killian snorted. "So it's you. Thought I recognized you through the window. What d'you want? And how did you know where to find me?"

Cap'n Mike smiled. "As to the second, I got some excellent spies working for me now, Jim. As to the first, you know right well what I want."

"You ain't gonna get it, Mike O'Shannon. I didn't leave town for my health. I left for a good reason, and I'm going to stay lost. So get back in the car with them kids and get out of here. Otherwise, I reckon I'll have to yell for a cop."

"You won't do that," Cap'n Mike said shrewdly. "If you'd wanted a cop, you could have got one in Seaford. Come on, Jim, and stop acting like you were the only one knew anything. We know what you saw the night Tom was wrecked. And we know who did it."

That stopped Captain Killian. He gave Cap'n Mike a penetrating look, then said abruptly, "Where can we talk?"

"In the car."

Cap'n Mike introduced the boys to Killian. "Rick and Scotty," he explained, "figured out what must have happened to Tom Tyler. Tell him, Rick."

Rick outlined the theory quickly.

Captain Killian sat staring out of the window. "That's about it," he said finally. "It must be. Maybe Bill Lake thought he'd lost the light and current set him over, but I was closer. Not close enough to see anything but the light, you understand. But I saw it blink out, and I looked down at the binnacle and held the same compass heading until it came on again, and it was in a different place."

"If you'd said that at the hearing this morning, Tom Tyler might have been free right now," Cap'n Mike accused.

Captain Killian's back stiffened. "I don't know what you're thinking, Mike, but if it weren't for Tom, I wouldn't be here."

"We'd like to hear about that," Cap'n Mike said.

"May as well tell you. Soon as I saw what happened to the Sea Belle, I hurried to find Tom. While I was looking for him, I ran into Brad Marbek and I asked him about the light. I knew he'd been right behind Tom. Brad acted mighty queer, and when I did see Tom, he got all excited. He begged me to leave town, for my own sake and his. I told him he'd have a hard time without my testimony and Brad's, and he broke down and told me Brad was mixed up in some kind of deal with them Kelsos, and he said he wasn't worried about himself, but about Celia-- that's his wife--and their little girl. He said he didn't dare try and clear himself, though he knew right well what had happened."

Captain Killian shrugged. "What could I do? Stay and put Celia and their little girl in danger? Not likely I'd do that! And I couldn't pretend not to know anything because I'd already talked to Brad."

The four nodded their understanding.

"So I packed up and got out. First I told Chick what to say, and told him to tell folks I'd been to the trawler next morning so they wouldn't connect my going with Tom's wreck."

"Was just the shifting of the light all you saw?" Rick asked.

"That's all. I will say that I knew the second light was the real one. I hadn't known the first one wasn't real, but when Smugglers' Light came on I could see there was a difference. I'd figured the light was sort of dull because of ground haze. There was some, you know."

"There's our evidence," Scotty said.

"Yep." Cap'n Mike leaned back in the seat. "Only trouble is, we can't use it without getting both Jim and Tom's family in danger. So I guess we're back where we started."

"But we can prove to the police the light was changed," Jerry began. "If Captain Killian tells his story ..." He stopped. "No good. Because we have no proof the Kelsos were mixed up in it, and they'd still be able to carry out their threats."

"That's exactly right," Captain Killian said. "Now how about telling me how you found me? Did Chick give me away?"

"Not on purpose," Cap'n Mike assured him. "Rick was trailing him when he telephoned you this morning, and he found out the number Chick had called. The rest was easy."

"I see. And what am I supposed to do now?"

"I don't see how you can stay in that hotel," Cap'n Mike said, a little distastefully.

Captain Killian smiled. "Pretty bad, all right. You know, last time I spent a night in New York I stayed there. It was right nice. There was a real pretty garden out in back."

"How long ago was that?" Rick queried.

The fisherman hesitated. "Oh, must be all of twenty-five years ago. I was some upset when I saw the place, but I'd already told Chick to call me there, so nothing for it but to stay. Wish I could stay somewhere else, but it wouldn't be safe to go back to Seaford."

"Whiteside would be all right," Rick said. "You could stay there."

"I'd rather. But are you sure it'd be safe?"

Jerry spoke up. "Captain, I'm on the Whiteside Morning Record. I'll make a deal with you. Give us your story exclusively, when the right time comes, and the paper will guarantee your safety."

"It sounds good," Captain Killian admitted. "But when is the right time going to come? Maybe never."

"Sooner than you think," Rick said quietly. "Look, gang. There's only one way to crack this case. We know now we can't get Captain Tyler cleared unless the whole outfit is rounded up. So we'll just have to get busy and find the evidence we need. We'll start over again, and this time we won't go wrong because we know what to look for, and where to look."

"Fighting talk," Cap'n Mike chuckled happily.

Scotty laughed. "Do we dare put our heads inside the Seaford city limits again after what we did to Carrots? He'll be waiting for us with a squad of thugs and that little popgun of his."

94

"The popgun maybe, but no thugs," Rick corrected. "What will you bet he never even tells his father what happened to him?"

"No bet there," Jerry said, grinning. "I'll bet the same thing." He put the car in gear. "We may as well head back to Whiteside. First, though, we'll have to collect Captain Killian's baggage."

The captain spoke his agreement. "I'll take your offer, son." He shook his head. "You know, I'm real surprised at Brad Marbek. I knew he wasn't above turning a dishonest dollar, but I thought he had more sense than to go into smuggling. No matter how foolproof you think your setup is, if you start smuggling you're bound to get caught. Sooner or later."

"In this case," Rick added hopefully, "we'll try to make it sooner."

Chapter 15: Plimsoll Marks

Duke Barrows, editor of the Whiteside Morning Record, sipped slowly at his cup of coffee, nodding encouragement at Rick every once in a while. The editor, after a few words with Jerry, had taken Captain Killian to his own house for safekeeping. The captain could stay there, Duke said, until it was time for him to make a public appearance.

But the price Duke asked was to be told the complete story. At first Rick hesitated. With no proof of anything except for Captain Killian's testimony, which actually convicted no one, he was a little doubtful about making accusations. But when it came to keeping a tight lip, the editor was probably more experienced than any of them. Besides, Rick hoped that he might have a suggestion, so, finally, they put Cap'n Mike on the Seaford bus and the three boys and Duke retired to a secluded booth in the rear of a restaurant to talk it over.

Barrows traced circles on the plastic table top for long moments after Rick had finished. "You've been pretty thorough," he said finally. "What do you plan to try now?"

Rick shook his head. "I wish I knew. We could try to get to Creek House earlier next time the Albatross puts in there, but we know now they guard the place."

"How about spotting the Albatross from the air while she actually loads at sea?" Duke asked.

"Rick mentioned that," Scotty replied. "But how? We can't fly at night in the Cub because we don't have landing lights. And even if we did, we could only go out in moonlight because we don't have any night flying instruments."

Jerry looked at the editor. "Duke, you know the Coast Guard commanding officer in this area. How about getting him to send out one of his planes?"

"We could," Duke said slowly, "but I'd rather not. This is Rick and Scotty's case." He grinned. "Besides, I'm selfish. If the Coast Guard gets it, every news agency and paper in the country gets it from official sources. I'd rather have an exclusive we can copyright, then every paper in the country will have to quote us."

"It would put Whiteside on the map," Rick grinned in response. "Seriously,

Duke, I'm afraid that's not very practical. Besides, how would we know when the Albatross was going to make contact with a supply ship? We know when he's going to Creek House, because Cap'n Mike can see him. But Brad has already made contact when that happens."

"Let's take one thing at a time." The editor drew pencil and paper from his pocket. "What would you need to fly at night?"

Rick ticked them off on his fingers. "Wing landing lights, navigation lights, cockpit instrument light. And if we were supposed to fly in anything but clear weather, we'd need a bank and turn indicator and an artificial horizon. But even then I'd be doubtful. I've never had instrument training. I wouldn't dare take the Cub out unless it was a clear, moonlit night, so I'd have a good horizon."

Scotty approved. "That makes sense. And if we stuck to clear moonlight, the only things we'd need would be landing lights and navigation lights."

Duke made notes. "All right. I don't think you need to worry much about having moonlight, because the weather is pretty consistent at this time of year. Barring a ground haze or a local thunderstorm, you'll have clear weather, and the moon will be full by the early part of next week. Now suppose we get Gus to install landing lights and navigation lights on a rental basis? The paper would pay for that in exchange for an exclusive story."

"All we'd need would be good weather," Rick said. He had never flown the Cub at night. In fact, he had flown only once at night, and then it was in a much better plane and with an experienced instructor. But with good moonlight and a clear sky, it shouldn't be much different from day flying.

Duke continued. "Now the next point. How can we know when the Albatross is going to make contact?"

"I think we can find out if Cap'n Mike will help," Scotty answered. "We know it takes time to transfer the smuggled goods, whatever they are. That means Brad Marbek has to leave port earlier in the morning than usual, unless he wants to call attention to what he's doing. As I see it, he probably leaves pretty early, makes contact with his supply ship and gets his load, then he hurries to the fishing grounds and gets his nets over the side and is fishing when daylight comes and the others see him. If Cap'n Mike kept watch, he would let us know when Brad left real early."

"That's good figuring," Rick complimented his pal. "The Albatross would have to leave between half past two and three in the morning. Otherwise, he wouldn't have time to load before daybreak."

97

"It wouldn't take long," Scotty pointed out. "They have to do their unloading by hand at Creek House, but the ship would have cargo booms. Two cargo nets swung to his deck would do it. It wouldn't take any time at all."

Jerry consulted his watch. "We could go to Seaford tonight and make arrangements."

Rick shook his head. "It's Saturday. The fleet doesn't go out on Sunday. Monday will be soon enough."

"I have another idea," Duke Barrows said. "Suppose we take the State Police into our confidence?"

"But we haven't any evidence to give them," Jerry objected.

"No need. Captain Ed Douglas is a good friend of mine. I can put it to him as a friend, and not officially."

Rick rather liked the idea of having the State Police on their side. He had a great deal of respect for the young officers, and he knew that they operated with military efficiency, plus FBI criminology training. What's more, Captain Douglas was a good friend of Hartson Brant's, and Rick knew he would treat their story with confidence.

"I'm for it," he said finally. "Besides, if the State Police sort of co-operated unofficially, they could have their highway patrols watch out for the truck that is getting the stuff from Creek House. The patrol car wouldn't even have to go into Seaford. They could just keep an eye on Salt Creek Bridge, because that must be the loading point. Cap'n Mike hasn't seen any trucks on Million Dollar Row."

"Fine." Duke Barrows rose. "It's still early. We'll get busy right away. First stop Whiteside Airport to talk with Gus about putting lights on your plane. Then we'll drop in on Captain Douglas."

Rick felt better. The pattern was clear now, even though there were a lot of "ifs." If Cap'n Mike notified them, he and Scotty could fly over the Albatross. If they saw it make contact with some offshore ship and load contraband, they could return to Spindrift and notify Captain Douglas. Then the State Police could be on hand at Creek House to catch the Kelsos and Marbek in the act of unloading. And that would settle the smugglers' hash once and for all! The prospect of flying at night made him a little nervous, but he was sure it would be all right. The only thing was, although he could take off from Spindrift at night he couldn't land there, because the tiny strip gave no room for errors in judgment. He would have to land at Whiteside.

"This is on the Morning Record," Duke said as he paid the check. "And while we're working on this, I think I'll try to dig into Kelso's record a little, too. Never know what might turn up."

*　　*　　*　　*　　*

Sunday was quiet at Spindrift. Rick and Scotty swam in the light surf below Pirate's Field, sun-bathed for a while, and then walked back to the house. Hartson Brant was loafing for the day, too, and Rick had an opportunity to talk with him for the first time in several days.

Hartson Brant listened to Rick's story and plans, and agreed that any night flying must be done in absolutely clear, bright weather. Rick knew the fact that Captain Douglas was co-operating had swung his father's decision, and he knew that although his mother would be inclined to object, she would accept his father's judgment.

It gave Rick a comfortable feeling to know that the State Police captain was interested. Captain Douglas had agreed to go along with their plans during a long conference the night before. And Gus had promised to get the necessary lights for the Cub from Newark early Monday morning, and to have them installed by Monday evening.

*　　*　　*　　*　　*

Rick and Scotty helped with the installation on Monday afternoon. The hardest part was feeding the wires through the wings and fuselage. The wires had to be passed from one inspection port to the next, which required a great deal of fishing. But by five in the afternoon, the job was done. The Cub now carried a pair of landing lights, like auto headlights, one under each wing, and red and green navigation lights on the wings. There was a tiny white light on the tail, too, which would blink in unison with the colored wing lights.

As they landed at Spindrift, Rick grinned at Scotty. "Your head set firmly on your neck? It might get jarred off first time I try a night landing."

"I should have stayed in the Marine Corps and lived a quiet, safe life," Scotty grumbled. "When do we try these things out?"

"Want to go down and shine the lights on Creek House?" Rick joked.

"Nope. Wouldn't be safe. Didn't that phone call warn you not to fly over Seaford?"

The phrase hit home. Rick yelled, "That's it! Scotty, I knew there was something funny. It was in the back of my head and I couldn't dig it out. But that's it! Listen, why would the Kelsos object to our flying over Seaford during the day? All their dirty work goes on under cover of darkness. They must have

99

some reason for warning us!"

"Gosh, yes!" Scotty started at a run through the orchard. "Let's go take another look at those photographs!"

They ran through the house and up the stairs to Rick's room, and spread out on a table the enlargements Scotty had made. "Let's see," Rick said. "There must be something they don't want us to see. But where? We know there's nothing on the grounds, and we couldn't see anything in the house or garage from the air."

"The marsh," Scotty suggested. "Try the marsh, especially up the creek from the hotel."

Their heads bent over the best photo of the area and two pairs of eyes scanned the marsh grass. Rick pointed to an area on the Creek House side of the marsh, a short distance below the bridge. "There's something there, but I can't make it out."

Scotty straightened up. "Got a magnifying glass?"

"There's one in the library." Rick ran to get it, stopped to explain to his father that they might have an important clue, and ran back upstairs again. It was a powerful glass. He held it over the questionable area and details leaped to meet him. Wordlessly he handed the glass to Scotty.

The boy bent and studied the photo, then he turned to Rick with a wide grin on his face. "So that's it! Rick, this is their cache. They must park the stuff there until the truck comes!"

The marsh grass had been bent cunningly over the area in an effort at camouflage, but the magnifying glass clearly showed some sort of barge piled with wooden boxes!

"Let's go take a look," Scotty said enthusiastically. "Maybe it's still there."

Rick started to agree, then a thought struck him. "We'd better not. They'd see us, and they might notice the lights on the plane. We don't want to tip our hand." Then he brightened. "But they don't know Gus's plane!" He hurried out into the hall and called Whiteside Airport. Gus answered.

"This is Rick," he told the airport manager. "Gus, how's your plane?"

"Running like a watch. Just like my car. Why?"

"How's to borrow it for a quick trip south?"

"Now he wants to imitate birds," Gus groaned. "Don't you know it's too early to fly south?"

"Don't want to go that far south," Rick said.

"Come and get it."

100

Rick had no hesitation in asking the obliging Gus for the loan of equipment because he was always ready to oblige in turn. Several times, when Gus's plane was out of commission or not available, either because of engine overhaul or because some flier had rented it, Rick had taken the Cub to Whiteside for Gus to use in instructing his pupils. Furthermore, the island boats were always at Gus's disposal and he frequently borrowed one to go on a Sunday fishing excursion.

The short hop to Whiteside took only a few minutes. Rick taxied to the hangar and he and Scotty climbed out. Gus's plane, a light private job of a different make than Rick's and painted red, was standing on the apron. It had the name of the airport painted on the side in large letters.

Gus came out of the office and walked to meet them. He was a short, stocky young man only a few years older than Rick, and his slightly sour look hid a keen sense of humor. "I called my lawyer," he announced. "He'll be right here."

"Lawyer?" Rick sometimes had a hard time knowing when Gus was pulling his leg. "What for?"

Gus shrugged. "You're borrowing my plane when your own is in perfect flying condition. It must be for something illegal. You want my plane to be seen instead of yours. You want people to think I did it. So I asked my lawyer to come. I'll have a witness to prove I wasn't in the plane when the dastardly deed was done."

"What deed?" Scotty asked seriously.

Gus looked wise. "You don't trap me like that," he said. "If I admitted what I know, that would make me an accessory before the fact. Nope, I'm keeping quiet about this." He leered. "But I know!"

"Accessory!" Rick hooted. "You know what that means? Something extra and usually unnecessary."

Gus looked hurt. "I'll remember that next time you come in for an engine check and I'll put emery in your crankcase. Go on. Get in and I'll whirl the fan for you."

Rick and Scotty climbed into Gus's plane, grinning. Rick checked the controls rapidly, then called, "Ignition off."

"Off," Gus repeated, and pulled the propeller through to prime the engine.

"Contact," Rick called, and Gus pulled the prop. The engine caught at once. Rick warmed it, watching his gauges, then waved to Gus and taxied to the end of the runway. As they were airborne, Scotty took the speed graphic he had brought and checked to see that a film pack was in place. Rick banked around and headed for Seaford.

There was no buzzing of Creek House this time. Rick flew in a straight line, just far enough seaward so that Scotty could get a good picture. As they passed the cache area, Scotty leaned far out and snapped the shutter. Then he turned to Rick, grinning. "Still there. About ten cases. It looks as if we've got the goods on them."

Rick flew straight ahead until he was out of sight of Seaford, then he swung a few miles inland and returned to Whiteside. Fifteen minutes later they were landing the Cub at Spindrift, just in time for dinner. But first Rick made a phone call to the Morning Record, reported their findings to Duke and arranged with Jerry to pick them up at the Whiteside dock later for a trip to Seaford. They had to see Cap'n Mike to make arrangements and Rick wanted another look at the Albatross. He had to memorize every detail of its silhouette, otherwise he might find himself following the wrong ship when the time came if another fisherman decided to get an early start.

It was dusk when Jerry met them. "Got a message from Duke," he said as they climbed into the car. "He phoned Captain Douglas to tell him about the wooden cases you saw. The captain is going to keep an eye on the stuff, but he says it isn't enough evidence. The Kelsos could always claim they knew nothing about it and we couldn't prove they did. The stuff isn't on their land."

"Proof," Scotty said sourly. "Golly, do we have to get pictures of them peddling the stuff to customers?"

"Just about," Rick commented.

  *　　*　　*　　*　　*

Cap'n Mike wasn't at home when the boys arrived. They parked in front of his shack and talked and listened to the car radio for over an hour before he finally appeared, then he greeted them tartly.

"Why weren't you at Spindrift when I phoned?"

"What for?" Rick asked. "What happened?"

"Brad Marbek's at Creek House again. That's what happened. I called to tell you, and your mother said you had left. What's the matter? Not letting what happened the other night scare you off, are you?"

"We sure are," Scotty replied.

Rick laughed at the old seaman's astonished expression. "Don't let him fool you, Cap'n. We've got another plan."

Quickly he outlined Duke's proposal and explained how they had outfitted the

Cub.

Cap'n Mike smacked his thigh. "Now we're getting down to cases. You just bet I'll keep watch on the pier so I can phone when Brad leaves."

"There's one more thing, Cap'n Mike," Rick said. "I have to get another look at the Albatross tonight. Is there any place from which we can see her without being seen?"

Cap'n Mike thought it over. "Yep," he said at last. "There is. There's a dredger tied up at the pier just south of the fish wharf, and Brad always berths in the same place, south side. I know the skipper of the dredger. We can sort of drop in on him and take a look from there. That suit?"

"That will be fine," Rick replied. "But we may have a long wait if Brad's at Creek House."

"Wouldn't be surprised," Cap'n Mike nodded. "Likely two hours. What say you come into my shack? Might be able to scare up a sandwich or two to pass away the time."

Rick looked at Jerry doubtfully. "There's a paper tomorrow morning. Don't you have to get back and help get it out?"

"Not tonight." Jerry grinned his pleasure. "Duke said to stick with you two and forget everything else. First time I've had an assignment like this. I have to admit I sort of like it."

"Good," Cap'n Mike grunted. "Then let's go see what we can find to eat. I got so interested in watching for Brad Marbek that I plumb forgot about food."

*   *   *   *   *

It was after eleven when the four left the shack and climbed into Jerry's car for the short ride to the pier. At Scotty's suggestion, they parked the car on the edge of town and walked to the dock where the dredger was tied up. They stayed in the shadows, hopeful that they would not be seen, and Rick thought they reached the dredge without attracting attention.

The dredge was deserted, but Cap'n Mike made himself at home. He led the boys into the wheelhouse, a small shack on the aft end, and they took places at the windows. They had arrived too early, as it developed. It was a full half-hour before the Albatross rounded the fish pier and steamed into her berth. The pier workers were gathered at the berth, obviously waiting impatiently. They had finished unloading the last of the other trawlers a full fifteen minutes before.

Rick studied the rigging of the ship as it approached and memorized the position of her running lights. The Albatross had only one distinctive feature; her crow's-nest, from which a lookout was kept for schools of fish, was basket-shaped instead of being perfectly round. The other trawlers, he had noted, had crow's-nests that looked like barrels. He knew he wouldn't forget the way the nest narrowed toward the bottom.

The Albatross was low in the water. As she slid into position and threw out her lines, he saw clearly the Plimsoll mark on her bow. The Plimsoll mark was a series of measurements in feet, running from the maximum depth at which the ship should lie in the water down toward the keel. By looking at it, the skipper could tell at once how much load he had aboard. Now, the top figure was barely showing.

Rick studied it, and his forehead creased. "That's funny," he said. He pointed it out to the others. "She's full up. You'd think she would be lighter after dropping off a load at Creek House."

"You would for a fact," Cap'n Mike muttered. "What do you suppose they're smuggling? Must be feathers. 'Cause if you added a few more pounds to the load she's carrying now, she'd be awash."

Rick felt a pang of doubt. Were they away off the beam on their guesses about the Kelsos and the Albatross? The ship certainly would be higher in the water had they unloaded cargo.

"Maybe they didn't unload tonight," Scotty ventured. "It would be smart of Marbek to just visit Creek House for nothing once in a while, to throw off any watchers. That way, he could make his story about visiting his relatives seem a little more plausible."

Cap'n Mike had told them that was the story Brad was handing out to those who dared question him about his visits to Creek House.

Rick's face cleared. "That must be it," he agreed. "But look, if he visited the Kelsos tonight, it doesn't look as though he would make contact with his supply ship for a couple of days."

"Suits me," Scotty stated. "I'm not overly anxious to go tooting off into the wild black yonder in the Cub, if you come right down to it. I'd rather Brad took his time, to let me get used to the idea."

He had stated so neatly what Rick was feeling that he had to grin. He had been wishing he had more confidence in his ability to land safely at night.

"Amen," he said fervently.

Chapter 15: Night Flight

It seemed to Rick that his head scarcely had touched the pillow when the ringing of the phone penetrated his slumber. The luminous dial of his watch showed quarter past three. For an instant he shivered. The ringing could mean only one thing.

He heard the creaking of his bedspring and the soft pat of Scotty's bare feet as his pal swung to the floor. Scotty had the faculty of waking instantly and moving into action. By the time Rick reached the hall, he was already lifting the phone from its cradle.

"Yes?" he said softly. "Okay, Cap'n Mike. How long do you think it will take him to get out past the fishing grounds? All right. Give us a call about breakfast time and we'll let you know how we made out."

The boys hurried to Rick's room. Rick snapped on the light and stood blinking in its sudden glare. "What did he say?"

"Brad just left. He was phoning from Jake's Grill. I guess that's the only place in Seaford that's open all night."

"My guess that he wouldn't go out tonight was certainly bum," Rick said. "The smuggling business must be good. How long did he figure it would take Brad to reach the other side of the fishing grounds?"

"About an hour."

Rick looked at his watch again. "That doesn't give him much time before daybreak. It starts to get light at about half past four at this time of year. Well, let's get dressed."

Rick slipped into slacks and a heavy woolen shirt, because it would be cold before dawn. Then he put on woolen socks and moccasins. He was getting his motion-picture camera from the closet when Scotty came in, fully dressed. Rick tucked an extra reel of infrared film into his shirt pocket and grinned at his pal.

"How's your nerve?"

"Mine doesn't matter," Scotty returned cheerfully. "How's yours? That's what counts."

"We'll soon know." Rick paused as his mother called softly. "Yes, Mom?"

He walked to the door of his parents' bedroom.

"Be very careful," Rick's mother cautioned. And Hartson Brant added, "Don't forget distances look different at night, son, even with landing lights."

"I'll be careful," he promised. "We'll be back in a little while."

He motioned to Scotty and then snapped out the lights and went down the stairs. He left the camera on the porch and they walked to the boat landing, hiking briskly because it was chilly. Their plan was to take both boats to the Whiteside landing and leave one of them there, to provide a means for getting back to the island after they had landed at the airport. Probably it would have been more sensible to have left the plane at the airport, too, but that meant a walk from the boat landing and Rick hadn't been sure how much time they would have.

In a short while they were back at Spindrift. They picked up the camera and walked past the orchard to where the Cub was parked, looking a little unfamiliar with the landing lights shining in the moonlight.

Rick stopped for another look at the sky. He had studied it periodically from the moment they left the house. There was a little fair weather cumulus cloud scattered here and there, but nothing that would interfere with visibility. There was a good moon, between a half and three-quarters full. Rick would have preferred the brightest of full moons, but he philosophized that he shouldn't expect maximum conditions.

A glance at his watch showed that slightly less than a half-hour had elapsed since the phone call. It would be another half-hour before Brad reached the probable contact point beyond the fishing grounds, and it would take the Cub only about twelve minutes to reach it. There was no use in starting just yet. He sat down on the grass under the wing of the Cub and hurriedly stood up again. The dew already had fallen and the grass was wet.

Scotty chuckled. "Something bite you?"

"Thought we could sit it out for a little while," Rick explained. "But it's too wet." He knew he couldn't sit still, anyway. He wanted to get into the air, to get the feel of things. "Crank 'er up," he requested.

He slid into the pilot's seat and placed the camera beside him. Scotty walked around to the front of the plane and started the engine. Then, as Rick warmed it, he untied the tie ropes, removed the wheel chocks, and got in. "Relax," he advised.

"I'm trying to," Rick returned. "Buckle in. Here we go." He fastened his seat belt and Scotty did likewise.

106

The grass landing strip stretched ahead for a distance that seemed much shorter in the moonlight. Rick glued his eyes to the point where it ended and pushed forward on the throttle. He wouldn't need lights for the takeoff. The plane shuddered and he released the brakes. The tail came up and the Cub rolled, picking up speed rapidly, then lifted smoothly from the grass. Airborne!

The horizon was clearly defined and Rick breathed a sigh of relief. No trouble in flying level now. Their only bad moment would come in landing. He climbed to almost a thousand feet, then set a course for Whiteside. He wanted to get a look at the airport approaches by night. In a short space he saw the field beacon and then the red boundary lights. He throttled back and let the nose drop, crossing the field at less than two hundred feet. It looked easy. The tension left him and he flew easily, automatically. He had been flying the Cub for so long that it behaved like part of him, without conscious effort. He climbed steadily in a shallow turn until his altimeter read two thousand feet and he was heading out to sea. Far below, Spindrift Island was a dark extension of the land, almost completely framed by silvery, moonlit water.

"Pretty," Scotty said.

Rick nodded. He knew his mother and father were listening to the plane's drone down there. They wouldn't sleep much until he was back.

They had spent ten minutes making the long sweep over Whiteside. Rick glanced at his watch, then banked around on the predetermined course. He put the Cub in a slow climb.

"We'll arrive a little north of the grounds," he said. "Watch for ship lights. We may see the supply ship before we see Brad Marbek."

"Maybe they've already met," Scotty remarked.

Rick shook his head. "They can't have met yet. Brad would have to go pretty far out. Otherwise, the trawlers going to fish would be able to see him and his supply ship on the horizon."

Scotty shivered. "It's getting cold."

They were climbing steadily. The altimeter read slightly less than four thousand feet. At that height, the men on the ships below wouldn't know what kind of plane was overhead. They flew in silence for several minutes, then Rick warned, "We're getting there."

"I'm watching." Scotty had taken the binoculars from behind the seat where they had been left. Suddenly he grabbed Rick's arm. "There. Dead ahead."

Rick banked the plane a little so he could see from the side window. Far

107

ahead and below, red lights and white lights twinkled against the sheen of the sea. Some distance separated the lights and he knew he was seeing both vessels. They had not yet met. His pulse began to pound a little. He pulled back slightly on the control wheel and let the Cub climb.

"We'll continue straight on," he told Scotty. "Then we'll turn and come back at a lower altitude."

"Okay." Scotty leaned out into the slip stream and put the binoculars on the lights. When the ships were behind, he pulled his head in again and rubbed his cold face. "That other ship is a freighter, but not very big. I'd say less than four thousand tons. It's probably a coaster."

Rick wondered, if it was a coastal vessel, why he hadn't found anything in the New York paper at the Morning Record. It was probable, he decided, that the ship was heading for some other port, maybe Boston.

"Funny," Scotty said. "The other ship is heading south."

"South? No wonder we didn't find anything in the shipping news. Listen, Scotty, what if that's just an American coaster? You know what that would mean? That ship would have to rendezvous with some ocean-going freighter, or maybe several of them." His voice hushed. "What if we've run into something that's only a small part of a really big smuggling ring?"

His ready imagination pictured the coastal vessel sailing regularly between Baltimore and Portland, Maine, meeting ocean-going smugglers and in turn supplying small contraband runners like Brad Marbek and the Kelsos all the way up and down the coast.

"I expected some big ocean freighter," Scotty remarked.

They had been flying steadily out to sea. Now Rick banked around so Scotty could look through the glasses once more.

"I can see them on the horizon," Scotty said, glasses to his eyes. "They've met. The lights are almost together. Hey! The lights just went out!"

"Probably turned out so as not to attract the attention of any passing ships," Rick guessed. "They can't see, as we can, that they're the only ships around. We'll stall for a while before going back. Give them time to get rigged for passing cargo."

He lifted the camera to his lap, then trimmed the Cub so it would fly by itself. Scotty took the power pack on his own lap and checked again to see that the dynamo-driven spring was wound tight.

Rick had connected the infrared attachment so that a switch was handy under his thumb when his left hand held the camera in position. The camera itself, run by its own spring, was operated by his right hand. He pressed the infrared switch and heard the dynamo whine softly. Scotty immediately wound it another half turn to bring the spring up to full tension again.

"Wish I had enough hours to do the flying," he said regretfully. "Then you could photograph without worrying about the plane."

Scotty had his license, but he had not yet accumulated the experience that would fit him for an adventure like tonight's, or rather this morning's.

Rick twisted the lens barrel, making sure it was full open, then he twisted the focusing ring until it stopped. Now the camera was focused on infinity. All he needed to do was aim and shoot. He looked at Scotty. His friend's face was a white blur in the dimness inside the plane. "Think we've given them enough time?"

"I think so. They wouldn't need much. The supply ship would have cargo booms all rigged and the first load in the cargo net. Better turn back."

Rick banked, letting the Cub slip as he did so. They lost altitude rapidly and he watched the silvery sheen of the ocean resolve itself into waves. There was not enough wind to make foam or whitecaps. The two ships would have no trouble coming alongside and moving cargo. He leveled off at five hundred feet on a course that would take them directly over the vessels.

Both boys strained to see ahead, and both saw the blurred outline on the horizon at the same time. Gradually the outline became clearer until finally they flashed directly over the two ships.

"Here we go," Rick said, and the calmness of his voice surprised him. He rocked the Cub up in a tight bank that would take them in a narrow circle with the ships at the center. His hands made delicate adjustments in the plane's balance so that it would practically fly itself. His feet were light on the rudder pedals. He lifted his hand from the wheel and the Cub held course without a waver.

"Now," he said. He took the camera and pressed it to his cheek, gripping it firmly. His eye found the telescope and he pressed the infrared switch.

Scotty's hand was poised, ready to grab the control wheel if the plane started to slip. The power pack was held tightly between his knees, and his right hand was on the winding handle.

The scene lighted up for Rick. He saw four men on the trawler's deck, looking up at him. He saw the cargo net suspended almost over their heads, and he saw men on the deck of the freighter. His right index finger pressed and the camera

109

started to roll.

The Cub held its tight circle and Rick kept his finger down. Then he felt the camera stop and knew it had to be wound. Swiftly he shifted balance and turned the winding handle until the spring was at full tension again. But his shifting of weight had disturbed the plane's delicate balance. He had to put the camera down and work the tab controls that trimmed the plane with his left hand while his right kept it steady.

It took a few moments. Meanwhile, Scotty had wound the dynamo tight once more. When Rick looked out, the cargo net was no longer in sight. The men on the freighter's deck were bent over another cargo net, working at cases that evidently were heavy. Rick kept the camera on them, shooting steadily, rewinding when necessary. Then he shifted his view to the trawler. The men were standing over a gaping fish hatch. Evidently they were stowing the first load while the men on the freighter prepared the second.

"I have enough," Rick said finally. There was nothing more to be seen, unless they wanted to wait for the second load to change ships.

"How much footage did you get?" Scotty asked.

"About fifty feet, maybe a little less."

"That ought to be enough. Let's go home."

Rick swung the Cub in a circle until they were facing the direction of the mainland according to compass reading, then he leveled off. "I wonder what they thought about the plane overhead," he said.

"It probably scared them stiff," Scotty replied. "Chances are Brad Marbek had a good idea who it was."

The one thing they had overlooked in their plan was Brad's possible reaction to seeing the plane, Rick realized suddenly. Great grinning goldfish! What if he really got scared? They might have defeated their own purpose by making him jettison his contraband!

Then he reasoned that Brad wouldn't dump his cargo if he could help it. Anything worth smuggling was too valuable to be dumped just because two kids saw it transferred. But still . . .

"If I were Brad," he said, "I'd get up a full head of steam for Creek House and unload that stuff. How about you?"

"Because you'd be afraid those two wild men in the airplane would report it to the police? Maybe you're right, Rick. We'd better get Captain Douglas and his men on the job right away!"

110

The street lights of Whiteside were in sight now. Rick took a bearing from them and swung slightly northward to pick up the airport. Then he saw the beacon. He had not bothered to climb after leaving the ships, so he passed over Spindrift at an altitude of five hundred feet. He knew his parents would hear the Cub and know he had returned this far safely. His palms were moist with perspiration and he had to swallow to clear his throat. Now that the moment of landing was here, his nervousness was returning. He leaned forward, watching for the airport marker lights and saw them directly ahead. The airport wasn't big or important enough to rate runway lights or a lighted wind sock, but those wouldn't have helped much anyway. He knew from watching the sea that the wind was negligible. And anywhere he landed on the field would be all right.

He throttled down and the nose automatically dropped to the correct glide position. Then, as he saw the red marker lights rushing to meet him, he threw on the landing lights. White swaths of light picked out trees and the boundary fence. The Cub flashed across into the open, dropping steadily. The ground seemed to come up appallingly fast, but Rick kept his nerve. It was only an illusion, he knew. The Cub was at the correct approach angle. But the illusion made it hard to tell when to level off. He waited a second too long, and his wheels touched and the Cub bounced. He threw power into the engine and the little plane lifted into the air once more.

"Tricky," he muttered when Scotty looked at him.

Scotty sat up a little straighter. "You're telling me?"

Rick went around the airport again and banked around tightly into the approach. His jaw was set firmly and he watched the field so closely that his eyes watered. He'd make it this time! He cut the gun and the nose dropped. He waited as the runway came up, trying to gauge his height by the grass that showed clearly in the landing lights. Slowly he eased the control wheel back and the plane leveled off. Slowly and more slowly. They were eating up runway rapidly. Scotty shot him an anxious look. Then, with feather lightness, the wheels touched. The tail settled gracefully and they were on the ground. Rick applied the brakes and the Cub slowed to a stop. He wiped his forehead.

Scotty leaned over and solemnly shook hands.

Rick gave the plane the gun again and taxied rapidly to the hangar, switching out his lights as he went.

Made it, he thought jubilantly. First night flight, safely over. And that's not all. We got what we went after!

111

Chapter 17: Enter the Police

Duke Barrows was waiting at the hangar when Rick and Scotty got out of the Cub. "I can see the headlines now," he greeted them with a grin. "Young Birdmen Fly by Night. Subhead: Get Up Early to Catch Worms Who Break Law."

"Speaking of getting up early," Rick retorted. He pointed to where growing paleness in the east announced the coming of daylight. "How did you know we'd be landing?"

"My house is near here," Duke reminded them. "I heard you buzz the field a while ago and I knew you must have gotten the call. So I dressed and came over. I hadn't gone to sleep after getting home, anyway. Editors of morning papers are night owls, remember. Well, how did it go?"

Rick reached into the Cub and drew out his camera. He held it up triumphantly. "The evidence is in here," he said happily. "We caught 'em in the act, Duke." Then he sobered. "But we're worried." He told the editor about their misgivings.

"Hmmmm." Barrows gazed at the night sky reflectively. "I agree that Marbek probably wouldn't throw the stuff overboard, but he might streak for port. I think we'd better give Captain Douglas a call. We want state troopers waiting at Creek House when the Albatross arrives."

Scotty groaned. "If they go now, that means we won't get any sleep."

"You hadn't better plan on going with the troopers," Duke said. "They probably prefer to handle things their own way. Besides, it might mean waiting all day. I'd say it was more important for you to get that film developed. I don't suppose you saw the name of the ship Marbek was getting his stuff from?"

"I didn't even think about it," Rick confessed. "I planned to, then when the time came it slipped my mind completely. I was too busy flying the plane and taking pictures."

Duke looked at the camera curiously. Rick had described it to him. "It's hard to believe that you actually got pictures at night. I'm anxious to see them."

"Me, too," Scotty agreed.

"Let's get organized," Barrows said. "First of all, how do you plan to get the film developed?"

"There's a lab in New York that gives 24-hour service. They can develop infrared, too. I hate to think how much they will charge me."

"Can individual frames of the film be blown up and made into decent pictures?"

Rick nodded. "The result looks a little grainy, but it can be done."

"All right. Give me exclusive rights to use the pictures and the paper will pay for them. Let me have the film and the address of the lab. I'll send Jerry to New York with them first thing this morning. Then we can have them back tomorrow. Is that okay with you?"

"Swell."

"Good. Now let's hop into my car and take a run over to the State Police Barracks. We'll get Captain Douglas out of bed and you can tell him your story. He'll know how to carry the ball from there."

Scotty got the binoculars from the Cub. He and Rick staked the plane down, then hurried to the editor's car.

The police barracks were just outside of town on the Newark turnpike. Captain Douglas was in bed, but he got up quickly enough when the sergeant on duty gave him the names of the three visitors. Rick described their night's work while the officer finished dressing. When he had finished; Captain Douglas, a strapping man who had been a Marine officer before retiring and joining the state force, nodded briskly.

"Good work, Rick. I want to see that film the minute you know whether your camera worked well enough for evidence. Now, m'lads, I've got to get to work. Instead of barging into Creek House with sirens wailing, I just think I'll put a pair of my boys in civilian clothes on the job, one on the water front and the other at the bridge. I have a pair of squad cars without insignia or state license plates that will be useful, and both of them are radio-equipped. The minute this trawler shows up, we'll know about it and we'll move in on them. I'll ask for a search warrant soon as I can get someone on the phone at the main office. How does that strike you?"

"It sounds all right," Rick said. "But where do we come in?"

"You don't," Captain Douglas retorted. "You go home and go to bed. The only thing you could do would be to hang around here all day waiting, because we couldn't let you go to Seaford and perhaps tip off the gang by accident. They must know it was your plane, and they're crazy if they don't assume you'll call the police. If no police show up and you don't either, it may lull their suspicions

113

somewhat. Tell you what. I'll phone Duke, or have the desk man do it, the minute we hear anything and he can phone you."

And with that, the two boys had to be content. Rick ran the rest of the film through his camera, unloaded it, and handed the can of film to Duke Barrows. The editor drove them to the boat landing. "With any luck," he said as they got from the car, "we may let folks read all about it within a couple of days. See you later, fellows."

Although it was scarcely daylight, Mr. and Mrs. Brant were already up and having an early breakfast. Rick knew it was just that they had worried about Scotty and him, and he felt a little thrill of pride in them. Even though they had worried, they had confidence in him and so they had let him go. He was glad that he and Scotty always had played square with them, sharing their adventures and discussing their problems.

Over breakfast, the boys related the story of their night flight while the Brants listened with interest. "It wasn't bad at all," Rick finished. "I did have one tough moment when we landed the first time, because I was a little too tense. But the second time was smooth as anything."

"I'm glad you went right to Ed Douglas," Hartson Brant said approvingly. "These kinds of jobs belong to the law, Rick. An amateur can go only so far, and then if he's wise, he calls the police."

They had barely finished breakfast when the phone rang. It was Cap'n Mike. He said that he had been standing on first one leg then the other ever since he first phoned, and would they please tell him what had happened.

Scotty obliged with a dramatic report and Cap'n Mike exclaimed his delight so loudly that Rick could hear him half the room away. Scotty hung up and grinned. "He's going to sort of wander over to that part of town himself, just to keep track of what's going on."

"Hope he doesn't attract any attention," Rick said.

"He's too smart for that. Well, what now? To bed to catch up on that sleep we missed?"

Rick couldn't have slept a wink, and he said as much. He was too wound up. "Let's go back to Whiteside," he suggested. "It's full daylight now and one of us might as well bring the Cub back."

"I'll do it," Scotty offered. "You've been getting all the practice, and you're the one who doesn't need it."

On the way over by boat, Rick reviewed again the events of the night. "Funny

114

that the freighter was heading south," he said. In the cold light of day, his speculation that there might be a whole smuggling ring up and down the coast didn't look too sensible. "Of course she may have reached there before Brad showed up and circled while she was waiting. We didn't hang around to see if she headed north again after they finished unloading."

"That could be it," Scotty nodded. "Probably is. Listen, what happens to the freighter if the police catch Brad with the goods?"

"Can't say. Ordinarily, I'd think the police would call for the Coast Guard to go intercept them. But we're not sure of the identity of the ship."

"We missed there," Scotty said. "Has it occurred to you that we're going to be the star witnesses if this comes to trial?"

Rick shook his head. "Not necessarily. If the State Police catch Brad and the Kelsos with the goods, they won't need us for anything. But if they identify the ship that supplied them, they may need us there."

"Unless it's a foreign ship."

"What do you mean?"

"They were outside the twelve-mile limit," Scotty pointed out. "That's the high seas. I'm not up on my international law, but I doubt if the United States could do much about something done by a foreign ship on the high seas."

"Never thought of that," Rick admitted.

He dropped Scotty at the landing, then turned the launch back to Spindrift. Once in his own room, however, he was too restless to do anything, even to sleep. He walked out to the lab building and sat down on the steps, looking out to sea. It was a beautiful morning. Soon as Scotty got back he would suggest a swim.

In a short time he looked up to see Scotty approaching from Whiteside. He watched critically as Scotty swung wide and banked into the approach over the lab building, then settled smoothly to the grass. He nodded approval. Scotty was a natural flier. He excelled at anything requiring a high degree of co-ordination between body and mind.

Rick walked to meet him. "What kept you?"

Scotty climbed out and they staked the plane down. "Jerry picked me up on the way to the airport. We talked for a while. He had the film and was taking it into New York."

Both of them walked with less spring in their steps than usual. Knowing that nothing was in sight but waiting was a letdown after the activity of the predawn

115

hours. But Captain Douglas had spoken and that was that.

"Wonder if we'll ever be able to prove that the Kelsos wrecked the Sea Belle?" Rick mused. "Even if the police catch them cold on a smuggling charge that won't necessarily tie them up with Captain Tyler."

"That's right." Scotty bent and plucked a sprig of mint from the patch next to the house and chewed it absently. "But we'll be able to show motive and method once they're in jail and Tyler can talk. And with Captain Killian's evidence, that will clear Tyler anyway. Why should we worry whether the Kelsos get caught for that as long as he's cleared? We'll have them on the smuggling charge."

"I guess so." Rick felt tired. "How about a quick swim? Then we can crawl into bed and take a nap."

"Good idea. What are we waiting for?"

The water was too good to abandon after a few quick dips, however, and they alternately swam and lazed in the sun until lunchtime. Only after a good lunch of several sandwiches and almost a quart of milk apiece did they feel like taking a nap. Then Rick said, "No word. I guess that does it. Either Brad is ignoring our flying over him or he has dumped his cargo. I'd like to know which. Otherwise, he would have put into Creek House long ago."

"Looks that way. But I'm too drowsy to care. Go on to bed and let me do likewise. We'll know soon enough what happened."

Rick undressed, drew his shades and crawled in, luxuriating in the comfort of cool sheets. But it wasn't easy to drop off to sleep. His active mind persisted in going over and over the events at Seaford like a record stuck in a groove, but after a while he slept.

He didn't even hear the phone when it rang. Scotty had to wake him. Then, drowsily, he and Scotty went down the hall.

"It's Mr. Barrows," Mrs. Brant called from below.

"I'll take it," Rick said. He picked up the phone. "This is Rick, Duke."

"Bad news," the editor said. "It's all over, and nothing came out of it."

Rick woke up sharply. "What? But, Duke, we saw them load!"

"Tough luck. Brad came in at the usual time and Douglas was waiting for him. They went over that ship from stem to stern and didn't turn up a single thing."

Rick realized that it was dark outside. Mother had let them sleep right through dinner.

"But the crates in the marsh," he exclaimed. "How about those?"

"Gone," Duke said. "There wasn't a thing but flattened reeds and muddy water."

Scotty had been holding his ear close to the phone. "Brad must have jettisoned his cargo," he said. "We didn't think he would."

Duke heard him. "Was that Scotty? Well, Rick, if the pictures prove out, we'll know he must have thrown the stuff overboard. Captain Douglas has faith in you. He says not to be discouraged."

"Thanks," Rick said hollowly.

"Oh, one other item of news; I talked with the agent who rented the Creek House to the Kelsos. They've given him notice that they're moving out next Saturday. What do you think about that?"

Rick's shoulders slumped. "Unless they try to pull something between now and then, we're sunk. Duke, do you realize this may have been their last load? We might have scared them off with flying over Brad and then having the police raid them."

"I'm afraid so, too. But Captain Douglas says they seemed pretty smug. They may try it again. By the way, Jerry says the film will be ready at five tomorrow night. I'll send him into New York early tomorrow and he can do a few errands for me, then pick up the film on his way home."

"Thanks, Duke," Rick said. He replaced the receiver and looked at Scotty. "Did you get all that?"

Scotty nodded silently.

Mrs. Brant called from downstairs. "I saved dinner for you, boys. Want to come get it now?"

"Right away," Rick called. "Thanks, Mom."

He and Scotty slipped robes over their pajamas and walked slowly down the stairs. Neither of them felt much like eating after the phone call. They had, with undue optimism, written the case off as practically closed. But now everything seemed as far from a solution as ever.

Chapter 18: Brendan's Marsh

Rick stared out the window at the gathering dusk. "I'd like to know what's taking Jerry so long with those pictures," he grumbled. "He should have been here an hour ago."

Scotty had been trying to read a book. He gave it up as a bad job and joined Rick at the window. "Maybe he stopped for dinner," he said.

"I'll put ground glass in his cake next time he comes to dinner if he has," Rick threatened.

Jerry had phoned before leaving for New York earlier in the day. After consultation with Duke, they had agreed that Jerry would bring the pictures directly to the island, and that Rick and Scotty would leave the boat at the landing for him to use.

The editor was as anxious as any of them to see the pictures, but, as he pointed out, there was no longer any special haste, and he preferred not to have both himself and Jerry away from the paper at the same time, especially in the very early or very late evening when the wire service newscasts were coming in.

Rick had agreed. He planned to project the film, choose the single frames that would be the most useful, rephotograph them, and make enlargements for Duke and Captain Douglas. The rephotographing was done with a special, inexpensive device that could be purchased at any photo supply store.

Scotty opened the window wider and stuck his head out. "Thought I heard something."

Rick looked at his watch. It was shortly after eight. "Let's take the glasses and walk out to the north side," he said. "It won't be completely dark until around nine, and we'll be able to see him coming."

"Wait a minute." Scotty held up his hand. "There. I thought I heard something. He's coming now. I recognize the launch motor."

Rick started for the door, then he hesitated. "You go meet him. I'll get the projector set up in the library."

He ran down the stairs and called, "Mother. Dad. Jerry's coming with the pictures." Then he hurried into the library, took his folding screen from the closet and set it up. He got the projector from its case, plugged it in, using his father's

118

desk as a table, and put on the take-up reel. He finished focusing just as Scotty and Jerry burst into the room. Mr. and Mrs. Brant were right behind them.

"Got a clogged gas line," Jerry explained breathlessly. "I finally got a man to push me to the nearest gas station. We took the gas line off at the carburetor and blew it out with compressed air. I didn't dare take time to find out what had clogged it, because I knew you'd lynch me."

"You're forgiven," Rick said. He had already taken the film from Jerry and was threading it through the projector gate. He inserted the loose end in the take-up reel and motioned to Scotty. "Here we go."

Scotty snapped out the light and Rick started the projector. White leader ran through the gate, then suddenly, clear as day, there were two ships below, their center sections brightly illuminated and the rest fading out slightly toward what had been the edges of the infrared beam.

"Excellent, Rick," Hartson Brant said. "Good work, son! That's much better than I had hoped."

"Same here, Dad," Rick said, eyes on the screen. The ships appeared to be whirling slowly, the result of his having taken the picture while circling in a tight bank. He could see the men on the decks clearly, and even thought he recognized Brad Marbek. Then, as the angle changed, he saw Marbek clearly, waving his arm.

"What flag is that?" Scotty asked suddenly. "There, on the stern of the freighter."

The flag was limp because there had been no breeze to speak of, but part of the design was clear. "I have it," Hartson Brant exclaimed. "That ship is of Caribbean registry." He named the country, then said, "Look for the name of the ship."

But the angle was wrong for that. The name was not within the camera's view, on either stern or bow.

The film was running out rapidly now. Rick watched the cargo net swing over, full of wooden cases, and drop on the deck of the freighter. For a moment it didn't register, then he yelled. "Hey! Ohmigolly! Did you see that?" He threw the reverse switch and the film ran backward. The net lifted from the deck of the freighter and swung toward the Albatross. Then he ran it forward again and watched the load settle to the freighter's deck.

Scotty yelled, too. "What a pair of chuckleheads! Rick, no wonder we didn't find anything on the Albatross and neither did Captain Douglas! They're smuggling stuff out! Not in!"

The Plimsoll mark! The Albatross had been heavily loaded because Brad Marbek had taken on the load at Creek House he would deliver later to the freighter.

That was why no ships had been listed in the New York paper as being in the right area at the right time. They had looked for arrival times, not sailing times.

That was why the cache of cases was no longer in the marsh behind Creek House. These pictures were of those cases being loaded on the freighter!

The picture ran through and white light flashed on the screen. Scotty snapped the lights on.

"We've got to get these pictures to Captain Douglas," Rick exclaimed. "I'll hurry and rephotograph them right away. It will only take a moment."

He hastily rewound the film while Scotty ran ahead to the photo lab. Hartson Brant said, "Ed will be glad to get those, Rick. But don't get your hopes too high. The pictures don't show any contraband in those cases, and that's what you'll need."

"I know, Dad," Rick replied. "But at least we know now why we've always been wrong. We were backwards!"

He hurriedly excused himself, then he and Jerry hurried after Scotty.

Scotty already had loaded the rephotographing camera with film and screwed a photo flood bulb into a convenient receptacle. It took Rick only ten minutes to select the frames he wanted to rephotograph and finish the operation. Then he gave the rephotographing camera to Scotty who wound the film all the way through and took it out.

"Let's develop it," he said, and reached for the shelf to take down a small developing tank.

"Wait!" An idea struck Rick. "How do we know Brad isn't going to load again tonight? Remember the Kelsos have only a few more days at Creek House."

Jerry snapped his fingers. "That's right! And I'll bet they're gloating over hoodwinking the State Police, too. They wouldn't be afraid to ship out another load, particularly since they know they're suspected of smuggling stuff in and it might be their last chance."

"We can't risk it," Rick said decisively. "We'll take this film to Whiteside and have the photographer at the paper develop it. How about that, Jerry?" The reporter nodded agreement and he continued, "While it's being developed, we can go through the New York papers again and find out if a ship of Caribbean registry is sailing. About midnight would be right for a sailing time."

Scotty reached for the light. "We'd better hurry." He snapped it out and led the way through the door. He and Jerry went directly to the boat landing while Rick ran upstairs and picked up his infrared camera, just in case. If the police raided Creek House tonight, he intended to be on hand.

Scotty had chosen the fast speedboat and already had the engine turning over. Rick jumped aboard and they roared toward Whiteside. At the dock they transferred to Jerry's car and sped through the streets to the newspaper office. Duke Barrows had just finished with the early newscast and, taking advantage of the lull, had gone home for dinner; he would return in about an hour, the photographer said. He was the only man in the office. Jerry gave him the roll of film on which Rick had rephotographed the critical scenes from the movie and asked for two enlargements of each.

"It's urgent," he said. "Duke will want to see these when he gets back."

"He'll have 'em." The photographer headed for the darkroom.

Rick and Scotty didn't wait any longer. They took the file of New York papers from the rack and hurriedly leafed through them to the proper dates.

"Here's one!" Rick found a pencil and jotted down the name of the ship and its owner. The next date disclosed a ship of the same registry and owner, but with a different name. They worked rapidly and it took only a few minutes now that they knew what to look for, and presently they had the job completed. Jerry, who had been phoning Duke, joined them and looked over Rick's shoulder as he read aloud.

"All the same company and registry. It's the Compania Maritima Caribey Atlantica." He stumbled a little over the Spanish name. This was good evidence. He looked at his friends, eyes shining. "Now for today's paper. Got it Jerry?"

The reporter found it on Duke's desk and they spread it out on a table. Three heads bent over it. There was no ship of that company and registry listed as sailing tonight. Then Scotty spotted a separate listing of ships now loading.

"Got one! But it's scheduled to sail night after tomorrow. And look! It's the same ship that was here two weeks ago!"

Rick sat down at Jerry's desk. He still couldn't escape the feeling of urgency. He had played his hunches before and he did so now. He leaned over and picked up a copy of the New York phone directory. With the others watching curiously, he leafed through it, found the right page and ran his finger down it until he had the number, then he picked up Jerry's phone and called it.

While the operator made the connection, he held his hand over the mouthpiece. "A hunch. The shipping offices are closed now, but the Port Director at New York will know."

A female voice said, "Port of New York Authority."

"Information on ship sailings, please," Rick requested.

The operator rang an extension and a male voice answered.

"I know you don't usually bother with information of this kind," Rick said, "but this is the Whiteside Morning Record and we need it for tomorrow's edition. I'd like to know if there is any correction on the sailing date of this ship." He read off the name and company and the pier number.

"Just a minute, Whiteside. I'll be glad to look it up."

Rick waited tensely.

"Here it is. That ship was supposed to sail Friday night, but the sailing has been moved up. She leaves tonight at midnight."

"Thanks," Rick said. "Thanks!" He hung up and turned to his friends. "Tonight's the night! I had a hunch something was up. Of course Brad and the Kelsos would have the sailing moved up, because they're frightened. I'll bet tonight will be their last load, then the Kelsos will clear out and Brad will go back to just fishing."

"Tonight or never," Scotty echoed. "What do we do now?"

"Call Captain Douglas." Rick picked up the phone again and asked for State Police headquarters. There was a little delay while the officer was called to the phone, then Rick quickly outlined their findings from the movie film and the New York paper. "If we get down there, we can catch them in the act of loading," he said. "How about it, Captain?"

Captain Douglas hesitated. "I hate to stick my neck out again after last night, but this looks like a sure thing. We'll need a search warrant, Rick, and it will take a little time to root out a judge. And I'll have to see the pictures first. We have to show cause when we get a warrant, you know, and the judge will be a little reluctant after last night."

"The pictures are being printed now," Rick told him. "You can have them in a little while."

"Right. I'll round up the men I need and bring them with me. And I'll get the judge on the phone and ask him to make out the warrant and promise to show him the evidence when I pick it up."

"How long will it take?" Rick asked.

"We'll be on our way in an hour. I'll get going right now."

The captain hung up. Rick looked at his watch and then at the rapidly fading light outside. "They won't be in time," he said desperately. "If they rush the loading, they can have the Albatross out of there. Then what happens? They'll have to get another warrant to search the trawler at the pier, and there won't be any evidence to tie the cargo up with the Kelsos!"

Scotty held up the infrared camera. "Unless we get it," he said.

Rick's eyes widened. Go back to Creek House? But even as he shuddered at the thought of what would happen to them if they were caught again, he knew there was no other way.

"Jerry," he said crisply, "we're going on ahead. Run us down to the dock and we'll get started. Then you come back here and wait for Captain Douglas and Duke. Give them the pictures and this dope from the shipping news, and for the love of Rick and Scotty, tell them to step on it when they start for Seaford!"

Jerry protested halfheartedly as they sped to the dock, but they convinced him it would be better for him to wait and impress on the others the need for speed. He dropped them at the speedboat with a plea to be careful, then headed back to the office.

Scotty got behind the wheel while Rick cast off and they roared out to sea with the throttle wide open. The speedboat climbed to the step and planed along like a racer, leaving a foaming wake. Then, as they passed Spindrift Island and met rougher water, it began to bounce from one wave crest to the next. Spray swirled over the windshield and into the boat. Scotty started the wipers. Rick crouched down under the dashboard and rechecked his camera, trying out the infrared dynamo and the camera motor. Just to be on the safe side, he had brought the camera case, which contained the extra film and a tripod. Now he got the tripod ready but waited to see what would happen before he placed the camera on it.

He sat back in the seat, satisfied that everything was in readiness, and looked around him. Suddenly he stiffened. There were ship running lights on the horizon. The trawler fleet was returning to Seaford, and Brad Marbek would be among them! He leaned over and switched out their own running lights.

Scotty glanced around, saw the masthead lights, and nodded his understanding.

"Better make a plan," he suggested. "What do we do when we get there?"

"Stick our heads into the lion's mouth," Rick replied unhappily. "I hate to try getting into the Creek House grounds again after last time!"

"Do we have to? How about watching from the boat?"

"We couldn't get near enough without being seen. Wait! We could at that!" Rick struggled to remember details of the photo they had taken showing the marsh opposite Creek House. "We could go into the marsh. Remember that inlet nearest the creek? That branched off in the right direction. There are emergency oars in this and we could use them as poles and shove our way in. We might get close enough."

"And if we don't, we can wade the rest of the way." Scotty leaned over and wiped mist from the windshield. "Good idea." He laughed, without mirth. "Brad and the two redheads would have a fine time chasing us through the swamp. Here's one pigeon they'd never catch."

"Make it two pigeons," Rick corrected.

They were making good time, even though the slapping of the speedboat over the rough water was giving them a bad jouncing. They roared past the last group of summer cottages before Brendan's Marsh, leaving a wake that set the boats anchored near the shore to rocking.

At Rick's suggestion, Scotty throttled down as they swept along the edge of the marsh. The noise of the wide-open engine might be heard at Creek House and arouse suspicion. Then, as Smugglers' Light neared and they knew they were getting close, Scotty throttled down still more. Rick unlashed the pair of oars from their position along the gunwale and got them ready. It was fully dark now and difficult to see, although the moon was rising.

Scotty leaned over and cut the ignition. "Don't dare to use the engine any nearer than this," he said, his voice low.

Rick saw that they were perilously near the creek mouth. He turned to look at the incoming trawlers and saw the nearest one almost abeam of them a quarter mile out. "Watch for that inlet," he whispered. "And let's get into the next seat back. The windshield will interfere if we try to paddle from here." He hadn't rigged the oarlocks, knowing they would be unable to row in the narrow inlet. They would have to use the oars as paddles.

They climbed over the seat back and each took an oar, kneeling like canoeists. Rick was on the inland side, and he saw the inlet mouth first. "Here," he whispered, and backed water with his oar. The bow of the boat swung around.

Rushes and marsh grass scraped past them. The lights of Creek House were still invisible. Rick strained his eyes to see; it was almost inky black in the tall

124

rushes. Then Scotty reached out and felt with his oar.

"Left turn," he whispered. He had found the inlet branch that led toward the hotel. Now he backed water, trying not to splash, while Rick poled ahead. The boat swung into the narrow channel, reeds touching it on both sides and making a hissing noise as they progressed.

"Only a few feet of water," Rick said softly. "And mud at the bottom." Each time he lifted his oar he felt the weight of a ball of muck on the end.

The boat slid gently to a stop. Both boys put their weight on the oars, but it moved only two feet ahead then stopped once more. They put their heads together and discussed it in a low whisper because they were near the creek.

"We're aground," Scotty said.

"Guess we get out and walk," Rick returned. "Better take our shoes and socks off. It will be muddy."

"We'll be lucky if we don't sink in up to our necks."

Scotty took his arm suddenly. Rick started to ask what was the matter, then he heard it, too. The cough of a Diesel engine exhaust and the clanking of gear told him that a ship was nearing. A shiver ran through him. Brad Marbek, coming in to load!

"Let's step on it, he whispered. He sat down and removed his shoes and socks, then climbed up on the gunwale and walked forward, brushing against the rushes but trying not to make too much noise. He took his oar and shoved straight down from the bow. There was about a foot of water, then another eighteen inches of mud before the bottom firmed. It would be hard going. He started back, but Scotty came to meet him, carrying the camera and power pack.

"The tripod," Rick requested in a low whisper. "If the ground is so soft I can't get a firm stance, I'll need it."

Scotty handed him the equipment, then went back and got the tripod. Rick screwed the camera into place with a few turns of the tripod nut. Scotty disconnected the power cord that led from the power pack to the camera and coiled it up. They could reconnect it when they needed it. Meanwhile, it would interfere with their progress. He slung the power pack over his shoulder.

Rick put the camera and tripod on the deck, then turned his back to the creek and lowered himself. The water was cold and the muck seemed to reach up for him. He felt firmer ground under his toes and let himself go, then held his hands within reach of the boat as he continued to sink. He was up to his thighs when the ground finally held. He reached up and took the camera, holding it high in the air, and started forward.

Each step was an effort. He had to lift his leg high before each step, and the mud clung. Behind him, he heard the sucking, splashing, of Scotty's progress.

Then the ground began to get firmer until at last there was only a thin film of water and about a foot of mud. The lights of Creek House could be seen through the rushes now. He held up his hand as a warning to Scotty. They were close to the bank. In a moment he parted the reeds and looked through. Scotty moved to his side. The Albatross was tying up at Creek House pier, and Brad Marbek was just leaping to the dock where the Kelsos waited. But the boys were too far down toward the creek mouth. They would have to move along the bank. Rick gave Scotty a little push in that direction and Scotty understood. He went back into the marsh a few feet, then led the way.

It was easier going, but still far from pleasant. The muck gave every step a slurping sound, and it clung in gobs. Then the vantage point Scotty selected was reached, directly opposite the pier. They parted the rushes slightly and looked out.

The crew of the Albatross was climbing down under the pier. As the boys watched, they poled out a shallow-draft, broad-beamed rowboat about fifteen feet long. It was the barge on which the contraband had waited in the swamp.

Rick put his lips to Scotty's ear. "Wonder why Captain Douglas didn't see that?"

"He probably did. It wouldn't mean anything with the cargo gone."

Sensible, Rick thought. There would have been no occasion for the captain to mention it. He searched for a bit of firmer ground on which to rest the camera and found it. He began to worry about the hum of the dynamo. Would it be heard when they turned it on? And the filament of the infrared searchlight would be visible, too, against the dark background of the marsh. Did they dare try it?

The crew of the Albatross was in the flatboat--it scarcely could be called a rowboat--already heading upstream. The Kelsos and Marbek walked toward the house.

Good! That would give them a chance to try the camera. Rick waited impatiently until the boat rounded the turn leading to Salt Creek Bridge, then he sighted in on the Albatross , checked his settings, and started both the camera and infrared light. The dynamo and camera motor hummed quietly. He breathed a sigh of relief, surely that much sound would blend imperceptibly with the normal night noises. Peepers in the fresher water upstream made more noise than

126

that. He walked ahead of the camera and peered into the infrared searchlight. If anyone looked real closely, they might see it. He hoped the men on the opposite shore would be too busy to glance his way.

He switched off the mechanism and settled down to wait. His trousers were wet and heavy with mud, and his legs and feet were chilled. Mosquitoes whined around his head and little gnats settled down for a meal on his exposed neck and head. He began to wonder if it was worth it.

Carrots Kelso came out of the house, and he had his rifle. The boys watched as he disappeared behind the hotel, taking up his position as guard.

Each minute had lead in its shoes. Why didn't the boat return? And then, suddenly, it was rounding the bend! Rick moved behind the camera and loosened the pan-head. He swung the lens upstream. Scotty parted the rushes for him and he began to shoot. Infrared illuminated the boat clearly. He saw the faces of the crew, saw the cases stacked from stem to stem and even read their labels. Hummer sewing machines. He didn't believe for a moment that there were really sewing machines in them, but he couldn't guess their actual content.

He stopped shooting and rewound the camera while Scotty cranked the dynamo spring, then he took another brief sequence, stopped, and waited. No more now until they actually reached the dock and started to transfer the stuff.

Red Kelso and Brad Marbek came out of the hotel and he started shooting again, then he switched to a telephoto lens and took a close-up of their faces as they watched the boat draw near.

Carrots appeared around the front of the hotel and Rick got him, too, before he vanished again, patrolling the grounds.

The boat touched the dock. A crewman leaped to the place where Kelso and Marbek stood. There was conversation with much gesturing and pointing into the boat. Then the crewman jumped down again and motioned to one of his fellows. Rick started shooting. Clearly, as though it were day, he saw the two bend over something in the bow. They heaved upright and a chill shot through him. A man bound and gagged! Then they turned the man over to hand him up to the dock and Rick's teeth clamped on his lip so hard that he groaned.

It was Jerry Webster!

Chapter 19: The Fight at Creek House

Rick and Scotty watched helplessly as Jerry was carried into the hotel, then they looked at each other wordlessly. In a moment the seamen who had carried him returned, but Brad and Red didn't.

The one who had first reported to Brad, probably the mate or bosun, stood on the dock and called to the men in the boat. The boys could hear him clearly. "Let's get busy. We've got to load this stuff fast."

One of the men in the boat asked, "What they going to do with the kid?"

"Find out what he knows, then knock him on the head and shove him under the fish until we're out where we can dump him."

Rick and Scotty grabbed for each other at the same time. They knew without speaking what they had to do. Rick snatched up the camera, hauling it out of the muck recklessly. He pulled the power plug and Scotty reeled it in. They plowed through the swamp as fast as they could without making too much of a disturbance. Scotty led the way, cutting straight through the marsh to the boat, his highly developed direction sense showing him the way.

It seemed forever to Rick, but it was actually only a few minutes before they were climbing into the boat. "What do we do?" he asked desperately as he stowed the camera. "If we start the boat, they'll hear it, and it would take too long to pole out."

"Swim," Scotty said tersely. "It's faster. Get out of your clothes, but tie the laces of your shoes together and hang the shoes around your neck. We'll need 'em."

Quickly they stripped to their shorts, then draped shoes around their necks and slipped into the mud again. The water deepened rapidly and they began to swim with a noiseless side stroke. Rick followed Scotty, knowing that his friend was at his best in a situation like this.

They reached the edge of the marsh and angled along its edge, swimming strongly. Rick was in an agony of fear for Jerry. How had he gotten caught? And where? Scotty slowed, then stopped. The sudden feel of sluggish current warned Rick they were at the creek mouth.

"Watch the splashes," Scotty whispered. "We'll cross to the outside of the

128

fence."

For the next few moments they would be vulnerable if Carrots Kelso happened to walk to the bank and look across. It had to be chanced. Scotty started out and Rick drew abreast of him. They swam cautiously, making no noise or splash, reached the opposite bank safely and crawled up the beach until they were sure the fence hid them from any watchers at Creek House.

"Got to draw Carrots to the back side of the hotel," Scotty whispered. "Then we can get in through the creek side of the fence. But how?"

Rick thought quickly. If they could make some sort of noise on the other side ... but it would take too long to go over there and then come back again and it wouldn't be safe to enter near where they made the noise, anyway. He started to put on his shoes, and as his fingers touched the strings, an idea blossomed. "Hunt for a piece of rope or wire," he said swiftly, and began running down the reef, eyes searching the dark ground. Scotty went to the other side and began to search, too. Rick knew they would find what he wanted on the wreck of the trawler but hoped he wouldn't have to go that far. He was in luck. He stumbled over a loop of rusty wire, grabbed it, and heaved. It came free. Swiftly his fingers explored it. About eight feet. That was good. Probably it had been buried when the part of the reef nearest the hotel had been filled in with trash to make a parking area. He had noticed odds and ends of junk around. He ran over to Scotty and told him what else was needed and they both hunted until they found a jagged piece of metal that would suit. It weighed about two pounds, and it had holes along one edge, probably originally drilled for rivets. They unkinked the wire carefully, then Rick passed one end through a hole in the steel and made it fast while Scotty bent a loop in the other end and wound the wire around itself to make a handhold.

"You do it," Rick whispered.

Scotty put a hand through the loop he had made and gripped it tight, then he went as close to the hotel fence as he could without raising the trajectory too high and began to whirl the contraption around his head. Faster and faster he whirled it until it began to whine, then with all the momentum of his body he released it.

The missile soared away in a long, low arc, past the hotel and on. The boys waited, not breathing, and heard it crunch through the reeds on the far side of the hotel. They ran to the creek end of the fence and looked around. The men at the pier were looking toward the marsh behind the garage. Red Kelso was walking that way and Carrots was running, rifle lifted.

Scotty and Rick rounded the corner and ran silently to the front of the hotel. Now to find Jerry! Rick stepped to the front porch and tried the door. It was unlocked. Taking his nerve in both hands, he pushed the door open and stepped inside.

It was quiet in the hotel. He knew the layout; they had explored every inch of it. He led the way toward the kitchen, then flattened against the wall of the hallway as he saw the light streaming through. He felt Scotty brush against him. Rick leaned forward, keeping his face in the shadow, just as Brad Marbek, his curiosity getting the better of him, walked to the side door and stepped out.

Rick took a long step into the kitchen. No one in it. Then he saw a lighted doorway across the room. It was a good bet. With his eyes on the door through which Brad had gone, he trotted swiftly across the floor. Scotty was right behind him.

Rick smothered an exclamation as he saw Jerry. The reporter was seated in a chair, tied fast to it. The gag, a bundle of rags, had been stuffed into his mouth. There was a bad bruise over his left eye and another on his left temple. Rick was at his side in three long steps. He jerked the gag from Jerry's mouth, cautioned him to silence, and started to untie him. Scotty went to the window, which fortunately faced the Seaford side of the house, and leaned out.

Rick heard Brad call, "Find anyone?" Then a faint answering call. "No one here."

"Hurry," Scotty whispered. He went to the door and stood to one side of it, looking into the kitchen.

Rick tugged at a recalcitrant knot, then got it loose. Jerry stood up, hands still tied behind him. Rick fought with the knot and wished for a knife.

There were footsteps in the kitchen. Rick's fingers got a hold and he heaved. The footsteps came closer. Scotty crouched. Brad Marbek entered the room and stepped into a terrific roundhouse swing with all of Scotty's frantic weight behind it. Brad stumbled backward and fell, and he roared.

"They're in the house! Cover the doors!"

He got to his feet and his powerful legs drove him forward. Scotty stepped directly into his way.

The rope loosened in Rick's hand. He unwound Jerry, working as fast as he could. He turned just in time to see Brad's arms reach for Scotty. The fisherman's face was distorted in a snarl and blood trickled from his cut lip.

Scotty back-pedaled swiftly. He took Brad's out-stretched hands, and then fell

130

backward, feet lifting, catching Brad in the stomach. Scotty heaved. The heave and the smuggler's momentum shot him headlong. He smashed into the wall.

Scotty leaped to his feet. "Run!" he yelled.

Rick propelled Jerry into the kitchen, and as they started across the room he saw Red Kelso at the door. "The front," he called. "Hurry, Jerry."

The reporter was fast getting the use of his limbs back. Scotty led the way to the front hall and Jerry stumbled after him. As Rick passed through the doorway from the kitchen into the wide hallway he spotted a cabinet. He grabbed it and tugged. It came away from the wall and he stepped from under it, letting it crash at an angle across the passageway. That would hold Red for a few seconds. They sprinted for the open front door and met Carrots head on just inside the entrance.

Scotty dove at him. His shoulder caught the redhead in the chest and slammed him backward. Carrots' arms flew up and the rifle he was carrying sailed from his grasp and slid across the porch to the sidewalk. The boys started to pile out over him, then they stopped short. Two of the crew were pounding up the sidewalk, leaping to the steps, and they carried clubs!

They were trapped! "Up the stairs," Rick said hoarsely.

Scotty bent over the fallen Carrots and jerked him to his feet. "You're coming with us," he grated.

Rick was already halfway to the stairs. Red Kelso was climbing over the blockade in the hallway, Brad Marbek behind him. Rick stopped. "Hurry, Scotty!"

"Hostage," Scotty grunted. He took Carrots' arm in a Japanese wristlock and rushed him across the room. Carrots struggled, then let out a yelp. It was either go peacefully or break his own arm. "Run," Scotty commanded, and Carrots ran, up the stairs. Jerry followed and Rick brought up the rear. Their pursuers were gaining!

Rick's mind raced as he climbed two stairs at a time, reconstructing the plan of the house. He rejected the idea of barricading themselves in a room on the second or third floor; the halls would give their enemies too much room for a battering rush against the door. "The attic," he called ahead to Scotty, "and step on it! They're gaining!"

They crossed the second-floor landing and went up the stairs to the third. At the top of the third landing was a rusty bucket, full of sand. Rick knew, because he had been forced to dig through the sand. It was evidently a relic of Coast Guard occupancy, placed there to extinguish incendiaries. He pressed hard against Jerry's heels, hearing the thud of footsteps on the stairs behind him and the cries of "Get 'em" from Red Kelso.

Scotty, Carrots, and Jerry sprinted for the attic stairs. Rick paused long enough to scoop up the bucket of sand. He hurled it after him, straight into the faces of the smugglers and found time for a grin at their yells and curses.

The attic stairs led straight up, with no landing at the top. The door was ajar. Rick's trick had gained a little time. They went through it with seconds to spare, and Rick slammed it shut. "Find a light," he gasped. "There's one up here." He remembered a tiny bulb, high in the ceiling.

"Key," Scotty snapped. "In the door. Outside. It was there last time."

Rick opened the door and had a quick glimpse of dark figures rushing up the stairs. He fumbled for the key, jerked it loose, and slammed the door. With his shoulder against it he inserted the key on their side and twisted it just as bodies thumped against the other side.

Jerry found the light switch and turned it on. Carrots, lips drawn tight, was bent over in the judo hold Scotty had on him. Rick found a few old pieces of overstuffed furniture, too disreputable to have been moved or sold, and he and Jerry pushed them against the door.

"If we can hold out," Jerry said between swollen lips, "Captain Douglas will get here."

"If!" Rick echoed.

Red Kelso called through the door. "Okay, you kids. Open up and we'll make things easy on you. But if we have to break the door down, it'll be rugged."

The boys looked at each other. Carrots grinned. Rick didn't like the grin. He yelled back, "Try to come through that door and we throw your son out the window!"

Carrots turned white.

"Stop talking like a fool and open up," Kelso demanded.

"We warned you," Rick yelled.

There was a solid thump as shoulders hit the door. Rick cast a desperate look at Scotty. The door wouldn't hold long. Scotty winked at Rick and jerked his chin at Carrots' back.

"Out the window with him," Rick growled. He lunged forward and took the boy's legs. Jerry, who had caught the wink too, took his shoulders while Scotty kept a wristlock clamped tight. They rushed Carrots to the window and Rick let go long enough to throw up the sash. Then they lifted Carrots to the sill.

132

"Pop!" he screamed. "They're throwing me out!"

The thumping at the door ceased. The elder Kelso called, "Keep your head, Jimmy. They don't dare. They know we're comin' in, anyway, and if they throw you out they haven't got a chance."

Kelso had spoken the exact truth, and the boys knew it. They let Carrots slump to the floor. "Get close," Scotty said. He spoke into Carrots' ear. "One peep out of you and I'll break your arm. Listen. We've got to have help and quick. Who's the fastest runner?"

"Jerry," Rick said promptly. The reporter had been a sprinting champion in school. "Are you okay now?"

"Fine. What's your plan?"

A door panel splintered as shoulders crashed against it. Good thing there was little space to stand out there. The smugglers couldn't get much leverage. Scotty talked fast. "We'll unblock the door and open it suddenly, then, Rick, you dive into the mob. They'll be off balance because the stairs are steep. Jerry, you'll have to leap for it, over their heads, and try to get away." He was behind Carrots and his wink was concealed. "Carrots will help us."

"I won't," Carrots stated.

"You will," Scotty corrected, "and you'll say 'Pop, hold it a minute. They want to talk it over.' Just like that." He twisted his hand slightly and Carrots yelped.

Scotty marched him to the door. Rick and Jerry slid the furniture away. The door was close to giving in now, the hinges starting to pull loose. Rick put one hand on the key and the other on the knob, hoping he had interpreted Scotty's wink correctly. Jerry crouched to one side of the door. Scotty held Carrots directly in front of it and commanded: "Speak your piece."

Carrots did, willingly, under the pressure of Scotty's hand.

The thumping stopped.

"What do they want to talk over?" Kelso demanded.

Scotty nodded. Rick spun the key and jerked the door open. Carrots, all of Scotty's driving weight behind him, catapulted headlong and smashed into the men on the stairs like a battering ram. They tumbled down under the impact like a row of dominoes, and Jerry went out the door as though shot from a crossbow. His flying feet struck backs, legs, and spurned faces. He gained the landing in a mad dive, scrambled to his feet, and was gone.

The smugglers clambered to their feet, or tried to. "After him," Marbek bellowed.

Red Kelso had fallen backward, and his legs were almost at the door. Scotty and Rick grabbed simultaneously and heaved, sending the upper men sprawling again. Then the boys withdrew and slammed and locked the door. Jerry had had the advantage of complete surprise, and his momentum had gotten him past the men on the lower stairs. Rick and Scotty couldn't have made it after the initial shock.

They pushed the furniture against the door again and drew back. Unless help was near, they were done for. There was nothing more they could do except wait, and fight once the door gave. Rick wrenched the leg from an ancient and broken chair and silently handed it to Scotty. Then he found one for himself.

The banging had renewed almost instantly. Scotty went to the window and looked out. Rick joined him just in time to see Jerry round the corner of the fence.

"He made it," Rick said with satisfaction. Two of the seamen crossed below, but Rick knew they would never catch his friend. He turned to face the door.

"Closer," Scotty said.

They moved closer and took places, one on each side of the door, and waited.

Smash. And again, and again. Wood dust flew as hinge screws gave with a loud screech. The door was just hanging now. One more smash! It flew inward and Red and Brad charged, two seamen close behind them.

Rick met Brad Marbek with a lightning thrust of his chair leg, and the smuggler doubled up. But his great body could absorb more punishment than Rick could give. He drove forward, brushed aside a swing of the chair leg, and his arms locked around the boy. Rick groaned as the steely hug drove the air from him; he felt a hand loosen, and kicked frantically for Brad's legs, then Brad's free hand caught him behind the ear, stunning him. Rick slumped to the floor fighting for breath and consciousness. Across the room, the seamen had Scotty, grabbing for his flailing arms while Red Kelso stood back and shot punches at him. Then the seamen got a firm grip and held him fast. Kelso's open hand slapped, back and forth, until Scotty's head sagged.

Carrots crawled into the room, his face contorted, one hand on his ribs. He got to his feet and walked unsteadily over to Scotty. He swung a roundhouse right. Scotty's head moved an inch. Carrots missed, and the force of his swing spun him around and he almost fell.

Rick laughed gaspingly.

Carrots' face turned scarlet. He walked over to where Rick was struggling for wind and drew his foot back. "I'm goin' to kick your teeth right down your throat," he grated.

Cap'n Mike's voice came from the doorway. "I'd call that mighty impolite!"

Rick turned on his side and stared unbelievingly. The old sea captain stood rock steady in the door, and at his shoulder was Carrots' rifle.

He spoke calmly. "Only got one shot in here. You could get me before I had time to pump it up again. Found it on the porch and took me a few minutes to figure it out. Almost put a slug through my foot doing it. But I got it in hand now. Got one shot. Who wants it?"

Marbek took a half step forward and the muzzle swung to cover him. Cap'n Mike's finger tightened. "You, Brad?"

Marbek stepped back.

"Come toward me, both of you," Cap'n Mike said. "Rick and Scotty."

Rick crawled forward, under the line of fire. Scotty, suddenly released, dropped to the floor and did the same.

The smugglers stayed where they were, frozen by the calm threat of the old man's voice. "Been eel fishing," he said. "Saw that young reporter skate around the corner with two men after him. Then I noticed Scotty and Rick looking out, and I thought I better take a hand. Didn't know just what to do until I spotted this BB gun in front of the porch."

His voice hardened as Red Kelso shifted position. "But now I know what to do."

Far down Million Dollar Row, Jerry met the State Police cars. And as Rick grinned up at the Captain, he heard the welcome sound of sirens.

Chapter 20: Read All About It!

Jerry Webster came out of the pressroom with a bundle of papers under his arm, the roar of the presses providing a background for his chant. "Extra! Read All About It! Spindrifters Smear Smugglers! Seaman Shows Shootin' Savvy! Simple Sap Scampers, Saves Skin! Read All About It!"

Rick snatched one of the papers. "Thanks, I will. Hey, gang, listen to this!" He read the headline aloud. "'Seaford Gunrunners Caught.'"

Scotty took a paper, too, and read the subhead. "'New Night Movie Camera Supplies Evidence for Surprise Raid.'" He grinned at Jerry and Duke Barrows. "Very restrained. Not a purple adjective in the lot."

Captain Douglas let out a bellow. "Hey! You don't mention the State Police until the second line of the story. Call a cop someone, I want these guys pinched."

"Charge 'em with serving poison coffee," Cap'n Mike suggested. "Never drank such a brew in my life."

Duke grinned. "That isn't coffee, skipper. It's printer's ink with cream and sugar. Go on, Rick, or someone. Read the rest of it."

"Byline," Rick said, "by Jerry Webster, and under that it says copyrighted by the Morning Record . How did you copyright it so quickly, Duke?"

"Sent a copy air mail to the copyright office and enclosed a dollar. The letter will go out tonight. It's standard procedure. Go on, read. I edited Jerry's story so fast I didn't have a chance to enjoy it."

Rick read on. "'A Seaford trawler captain, four members of his crew, and two New Yorkers were arrested tonight on gunrunning charges after a surprise raid by State Police officers culminated a series of events that included the wrecking of the trawler Sea Belle , the use of a new invention by the two youngest members of the Spindrift Island Foundation to photograph the transfer of arms under cover of darkness on the high seas, the kidnapping and maltreatment of a Morning Record reporter, and a fight in the attic of the Creek House hotel that was ended by the timely intervention of a retired sea captain.'" Rick got the last words out with his last bit of breath.

Scotty looked at Jerry with admiration. "He's not only a distance runner, he's a

136

distance writer. That was a hundred-yard sentence."

"I cannot tell a lie," Jerry said modestly. "I did it with my little dictionary. Written by an ancestor who was also famous. Noah Webster."

"'One of the most surprising disclosures,'" Rick read on, "'was the reason for the stubborn silence of Captain Thomas Tyler, master of the trawler Sea Belle , which was wrecked on Smugglers' Reef a week ago. As reported in previous editions, Captain Tyler maintained an obstinate silence as to the real reason for the wreck of the trawler in the face of pleas from friends and officials. He had maintained that he was solely responsible and that his error in judgment had been caused by liquor. After the arrest of the smugglers, Captain Tyler willingly told this reporter that he had discovered the smuggling activities of Captain Bradford Marbek and Roger and James Kelso two weeks before.'"

"That was a good guess we made," Cap'n Mike said soberly. "Poor Tom. He was in some spot. He knew about the smuggling, but he was like we were. Couldn't prove a thing. He could have told the police and asked for protection, but they wouldn't have had grounds for holding Brad and the Kelsos. They would have been free to carry out their threats against his family inside of twenty-four hours."

"That's right," Scotty said. "But he didn't know any more than we did what they were smuggling."

The axes of police officers had disclosed rifles, submachine guns, and ammunition in the cases innocently labeled as sewing machines, and no one had been more surprised than the boys.

"Thousands of guns and ammunition must have gone out before we caught on," Rick said. "What happens to the people that received them?"

"That's not our affair," Captain Douglas told him. "Since they went to ships and nationals of a foreign country, it's up to the Department of State to take action, if there's going to be any."

"We filed the story with Universal Press Service," Jerry explained. "It's all over the country by this time. Copyright by the Whiteside Morning Record ." He grinned. "We're modest, Duke and I."

"You are, anyway," Rick scoffed. "'Kidnapping and maltreatment of a Morning Record reporter.' Why didn't you give the reporter's name?"

Jerry turned a little red, but he said loftily, "We heroes prefer to remain anonymous."

"Heroes is right," Duke said dryly. "You came within an inch of having a

137

bronze plaque erected to your memory as one who fell in line of duty."

"What? Only bronze?" Jerry looked hurt.

Rick gave him a comradely wink. Jerry's act had brought him close to the ranks of heroes at that, if quick thinking and nerve combined with bad luck were any qualification. He glanced through the story quickly, and found what the young reporter had said about his own part.

"'While attempting to gather evidence, the Morning Record reporter who figured in the case was caught by the truckmen who delivered the arms to Creek House. After being beaten, bound, and gagged, he was taken to the hotel. His questioning was interrupted by the arrival of Brant and Scott.'"

And that really was modesty. Jerry had been returning from the boat landing when he passed a big trailer truck that carried the name of a large manufacturer of industrial castings. He thought quickly, surprised at seeing such a vehicle in Whiteside. Such trucks always used the shorter main route. To his positive knowledge, there was not a single manufacturing plant on the entire shore road on which Whiteside and Seaford were located. There was a definite chance, he decided, that the truck might be carrying a load for Creek House. He knew the smugglers had made fast changes in their plans, as witness the moving up of the ship sailing. There was a strong possibility they had been forced to ask for immediate shipment of contraband, too.

Jerry passed the truck and stopped at the newspaper long enough to scrawl a note to Duke, explaining what had happened, then he passed the truck again and drove furiously toward Seaford. He went by Salt Creek Bridge and parked his car in a pasture, then ran back to the bridge, made his way into the marsh and waited.

The trailer truck arrived, stopped, and put out flares, and three men got out. They jacked up the rear wheels of the trailer, then started to unload. By so doing, they had a perfect reason for being there. If a police car came along, they had only to explain that they had broken an axle and were replacing it, and that they had taken out part of their cargo to lighten the load until repairs were completed.

The stage was no sooner set than up the river came the flatboat from Creek House. It pushed its way into the marsh, toward Jerry. Not until the actual loading started did he discover his bad luck. He had taken a fairly well-defined path into the marsh. The path was artificial, made by the Kelsos. They had carried rocks to make both the path and the stone jetty to which the flatboat had come. The deception had worked, because the path and jetty surfaces, strong enough to carry the weight of men with heavy cases, were under an inch of mud and water!

Jerry had described the end simply. "They fell over me. I tried to get away, but there were too many of them."

But he had gotten in one good blow. His hand closed over one of the rocks of the path and he swung it effectively. The State Police, hearing his story, made a routine check of doctors and hospitals along the route the truck probably had taken; they assumed it would not turn around on the narrow shore road. The trucker Jerry had felled was in a small clinic two towns below Seaford, and an interstate alarm had gone out for the others, giving license numbers and descriptions supplied by the reporter. They wouldn't get far.

Jerry's luck had been bad, but Captain Douglas' luck had been good. The accumulated evidence probably would have been enough, but one of Brad's seamen had talked, hoping for a lighter sentence.

Rick was most pleased to find that his theory about Smugglers' Light had been close to the truth. The marks on the old tower had been made by a powerful light supplied by Brad Marbek. The light, once used for night purse seine fishing, was powered by a carbon arc. A cable, connected into the same junction box that supplied Smugglers' Reef Light, had furnished the power. The police officers had found signs of tampering in the junction box, but they had called the authorities responsible for the light to make a definite check. The light itself had been stowed in Brad Marbek's home. One quarter of the cylinder had been blacked out with paint. Red cellophane was pasted on to another quarter.

There were still no answers to who had phoned the warning to Rick, or why Carrots had trailed them into Whiteside, but those things weren't important, anyway. Probably their original guesses had been right.

The others had fallen silent, engrossed in reading Jerry's story. Rick went through it again, more carefully. The young reporter had done well. It was an exciting yarn. Then he looked at the "side pieces," other stories dealing with the case, written by both Duke and Jerry in the feverish rush to make the morning paper. There was a simple statement by Captain Killian, who long since was asleep in his own bed at Seaford. There was a photo of Rick and Scotty with the infrared camera and a story by Duke of its use in the collecting of evidence. The staff photographer had taken that one after they all returned to Whiteside, accompanying the police and the prisoners to jail. The entire back page was devoted to pictures, some reproductions from Rick's movie and some taken at the jail by the staff photographer. There was one of Cap'n Mike holding Carrots'

139

rifle, and the caption explained how he had rescued the boys.

"How much per column inch did you say?" Rick asked Duke slyly.

"Too much. This will bankrupt me."

Scotty folded his paper. "We'd better get back to Spindrift, Rick."

"That's right." Rick knew his folks would be waiting to see the paper, too. He had phoned them as soon as they reached the jail.

"I'll take you to the landing," Jerry offered, "then I'll run Cap'n Mike down to Seaford."

"Never mind," Captain Douglas said. "I have a patrol car going down that way in fifteen minutes. It can drop him off."

Cap'n Mike shook hands with both of the boys. "I'll see you tomorrow, I reckon."

"In the afternoon," Rick said. "We'll sleep in the morning." After the fight at Creek House, Cap'n Mike had rowed them to the Spindrift speedboat in his dory. They had gotten their clothes, but left the boat at the hotel. It would be safe; police officers would keep an eye on it while guarding the load of arms.

Captain Douglas shook hands, too. "I should make a speech," he told them with a smile. "You know, about your both being good citizens, aiding the police at risk of life and limb and so on...."

Rick grinned sheepishly. "I'm afraid we weren't thinking about the citizen part of it, Captain. We just...."

"I was about to add that." Captain Douglas laughed. "But thanks, anyway."

Duke Barrows said, "I don't suppose you would accept the coffee we served you as part payment?"

Scotty snorted. "Aren't you the one said it wasn't coffee?"

"All right." Duke's shoulders slumped. "Drive me into debt paying you off. Go ahead."

"We will," Rick retorted, "and don't take the price of these papers you gave us off the amount, either."

The editor laughed. "Okay. Take them home, Jerry. They'll have to wait until the first of the month for their money, just like the rest of our creditors. So long, kids, and thanks a million for a swell story."

As they drove to the landing, Rick glanced quizzically at Jerry. "Well, you asked for it. Remember?"

Jerry was puzzled.

"The night we went to get a story on the wreck," Scotty explained. "Didn't you say you wished you would get in on an adventure with us?"

"I certainly did. I didn't know what I was asking for, believe me." Jerry's grin widened. He touched his head tenderly, patting the bruises he had collected. Then he laughed. "I was scared silly, but you know, I kind of enjoyed it!"

Rick and Scotty broke into laughter, too.

*   *   *   *   *

Rick was figuring out some changes in the infrared camera attachment on the following Monday when Scotty came into the room.

"Just got back from Whiteside with the paper and the mail," he announced. "And look at this!" He indicated an item on the front page.

It was a Universal News Service dispatch. Authorities of a republic in the Caribbean had arrested the country's former dictator on a charge of planning a revolution, pointing to a large cache of arms and ammunition found on his estate as evidence. Arrested for complicity was the president of the Compania Maritima Caribey Atlantica. Warrants were being issued for a number of others.

"That settles that," Rick said. "Looks like we stopped a revolution!"

"We're the kids what did it," Scotty boasted. He dropped a letter in front of Rick. "Got this, too. Look who it's from."

The postmark was Bombay. It was from Chahda, the first letter since the Hindu boy had left them in New Caledonia to return to India.

"He's fine," Scotty said. "I read it at the post office. His brothers and sisters didn't believe some of his stories, but he's convincing them. Also, he's going to work. He can't tell us yet what his job will be, because it's a sort of secret."

"Then he won't come back to America for a while," Rick said, disappointed. "We won't see him." He grinned, remembering the first time they had met Chahda. "He's probably at Crawford Market right now, bargaining at the top of his lungs for something." He picked up the letter and started to read, picturing Chahda, in his native dress once more, at home in Bombay.

*   *   *   *   *

Rick's mental image was far from the truth. As he read the letter, Chahda was writing to Rick and Scotty again, but this time he was composing an urgent cable, laboriously working over the cipher that would conceal its content from his strange enemy.

The Hindu boy was in the hiding place he had chosen deep in the Indian quarter of Singapore, but he knew it was only a temporary refuge. Once he emerged, the shadow would find him again. But if he could succeed in getting to the cable office first, Rick and Scotty would get his message, and they would come. Once the three of them were united again, let the shadow do as it would!

Chahda finished his composition, folded it and tucked it securely into his turban, then he slipped through a door into the darkness of the Singapore night. In his ciphered message was the key to an adventure that would plunge his American friends into both darkness and danger in the fabled, terrifying Caves of Korse Lenken, a story to be related in the next volume,

The Caverns of Fear